THE VANDERBEEKERS
and the HIDDEN GARDEN

By Karina Yan Glaser

HOUGHTON MIFFLIN HARCOURT
BOSTON NEW YORK

hmhbooks.com

The text was set in Stempel Garamond.

The Library of Congress has cataloged the hardcover edition as follows:
Names: Glaser, Karina Yan, author.
Title: The Vanderbeekers and the hidden garden / by Karina Yan Glaser.
Description: Boston ; New York : Houghton Mifflin Harcourt, [2018] |
Series: The Vanderbeekers ; 2 | Summary: "When catastrophe strikes their beloved
upstairs neighbors, the Vanderbeeker children set out to build the best, most
magical healing garden in Harlem—in spite of a locked fence, thistles and trash,
and the conflicting plans of a wealthy real estate developer." —Provided by
publisher. Identifiers: LCCN 2018007637
Subjects: | CYAC: Gardening—Fiction. | Family life—New York (State)—
Harlem—Fiction. | Neighbors—Fiction. | African Americans—Fiction. | Harlem
(New York, N.Y.)—Fiction. | New York (N.Y.)—Fiction. |
BISAC: JUVENILE FICTION / Family / Siblings. | JUVENILE FICTION /
Lifestyles / City & Town Life. | JUVENILE FICTION / Social Issues /
Friendship. Classification: LCC PZ7.1.G5847 Vaf 2018 | DDC [Fic]—dc23
LC record available at https://lccn.loc.gov/2018007637

ISBN: 978-1-328-77002-8 hardcover
ISBN: 978-0-358-11734-6 paperback

Printed in the United States of America
5 2021
4500827416

For Kaela and Lina.

This garden is for you.

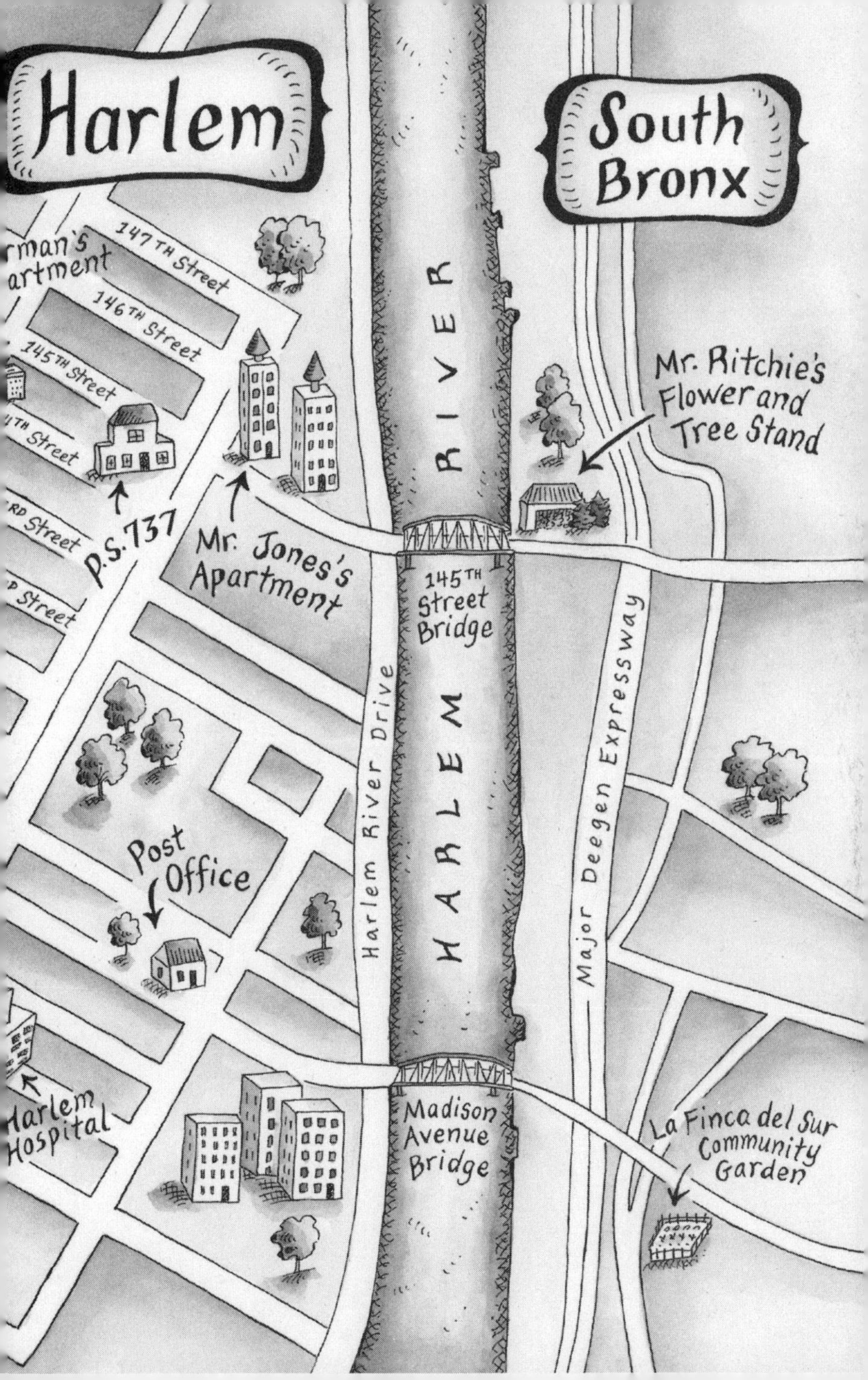
Harlem
South Bronx
147TH Street
146TH Street
145TH Street
Street
RD Street
Street
rman's
artment
P.S. 737
Mr. Jones's
Apartment
HARLEM RIVER
Mr. Ritchie's
Flower and
Tree Stand
145TH
Street
Bridge
Harlem River Drive
Major Deegen Expressway
Post
Office
Harlem
Hospital
Madison
Avenue
Bridge
La Finca del Sur
Community
Garden

"If you look the right way, you can see that the whole world is a garden."

-Frances Hodgson Burnett, *The Secret Garden*

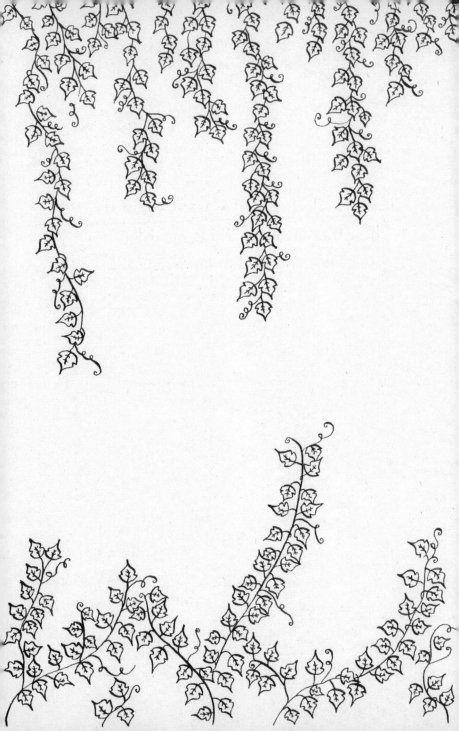

TUESDAY, JUNE 26

One

This is the most boring summer in the whole history of the world," nine-year-old Oliver Vanderbeeker announced. He was wearing basketball shorts and a faded blue T-shirt, and his hair was sticking out in every direction.

"It's only the first week of summer vacation," Miss Josie, the Vanderbeekers' second-floor neighbor, pointed out. The Vanderbeekers, who lived on the ground floor and first floor of a brownstone in Harlem, spent a lot of time on the second floor when their mother was busy baking for her clients. Miss Josie had her hair in curlers and was watering her many trays of seedlings, which covered the dining room table. When she was finished, she stepped over to a window box, clipped a few small purple flowers, and put them in a bud vase before handing it to Laney. "Bring these to Mr. Jeet, won't you, dear?"

Laney, five and a quarter years old and the youngest of Oliver's four sisters, stopped tying ribbons around the ears of her rabbit, Paganini, and stood up. She wore a silver skirt made of sparkly tulle, a purple T-shirt, and sparkly red shoes. The shoes were slippery on the bottom, so she shuffled slowly over to Mr. Jeet, careful not to spill the water in the vase. Paganini hopped close by her heels, shaking his head, causing his ears to flip around and the ribbons to launch in different directions.

"How are you bored already?" Mr. Beiderman asked. Mr. Beiderman was their third-floor neighbor and landlord, and up until half a year ago, he hadn't left his apartment in six years. He had almost refused to renew their lease back in December. But the Vanderbeeker kids had managed to convince him to let them stay, and now they were working on getting him outside the brownstone. He visited the Vander-beekers as well as Miss Josie and her husband, Mr. Jeet,

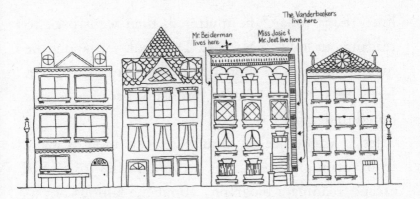

almost daily, but he had never left the building once in all that time.

Oliver slumped into a sunshine-yellow vinyl chair at the kitchen table, his elbows on the metal tabletop, his hands propping up his head. "There's nothing to do. Nothing I *can* do, anyways."

Oliver watched Miss Josie pull a shoebox down from a high cupboard and lift the top off. Inside were a dozen pill bottles. One by one, she opened bottles and shook pills into a cup. "And what do you want to do?" she asked.

"Text my friends," Oliver said immediately. "Watch basketball videos on YouTube. Play *Minecraft*."

Mr. Beiderman flattened his mouth into a straight

line. "Kids today," he muttered, then went back to reading out loud to Mr. Jeet. The book was about the history of roses in England. Oliver noticed that Mr. Jeet's eyes fluttered closed, probably because he was bored to death.

Jessie Vanderbeeker, who was a few months away from turning thirteen, was sitting on Miss Josie's fire escape, reading a biography about the famous physicist Chien-Shiung Wu. She leaned her head through the kitchen window between a curtain of ivy tendrils trailing down from Mr. Beiderman's planters above. Her frizzy hair caught onto some of the ivy, making her look electrocuted. "Oliver, seriously," Jessie said. "You're worse than Herman Huxley."

"Herman Huxley!" Oliver spluttered. Being compared to Herman Huxley was like being compared to gum on the bottom of your shoe or jellyfish in a lake on a beautiful summer day when all you wanted to do was cannonball off the dock into the water. Herman Huxley complained about everything, including cold weather, hot weather, and his brand-new Nikes, which any other kid would sell their most prized possessions for.

"Yup," Jessie said, whipping out her new-as-of-last-week phone and punching it with her thumbs.

Oliver felt a wave of pure green jealousy wash over him as Jessie flaunted her phone.

Jessie continued talking, her eyes never leaving the screen. "You know Mama and Papa got this for me so I can keep in touch with Isa." She disappeared back behind the curtain of ivy.

Oliver glared in her direction. It wasn't fair. Isa, yet *another* sister and Jessie's twin, had been chosen for some special three-week-long orchestra camp four hours away by car, but that didn't mean she and Jessie should have whatever they wanted.

Hyacinth, age seven and the sister who annoyed Oliver the least, spoke up from her perch on the armrest of Mr. Jeet's chair, where she was working on a new type of knitting using only her fingers—no needles. By wrapping yarn around her fingers and doing some complicated looping, she created a rope of yarn that fell to the ground. "Tell Isa I love her and miss her a million, trillion times. And then put that unicorn emoji at the end, and lots of those pink hearts." Next to her was Franz, her basset hound, who sneezed three times, then nudged Hyacinth's foot with his nose.

"Ha!" said Oliver triumphantly. "She can't even do emojis on that stupid flip phone."

"Language," reminded Miss Josie. She handed Oliver the cup of pills—there were, like, a hundred pills in there!—and a glass of water. "Bring these to Mr. Jeet, will you, dear?"

Oliver unglued himself from his chair and walked to Mr. Jeet. Mr. Jeet wore his customary crisp button-down shirt, a lavender bow tie, and ironed gray slacks. Oliver did not understand why Mr. Jeet *voluntarily* dressed up every day. He was a jeans-and-T-shirt guy himself; the dirtier the clothes, the better the mojo. After he put the pills on the little table by Mr. Jeet's seat, next to a framed photo of the Jeets' twelve-year-old grandnephew Orlando posing with a science-fair trophy, he dragged himself back to his chair and slumped into it.

"Why don't you play basketball?" Miss Josie suggested.

"No one's around," he mumbled. "Everyone's at camp. *Basketball* camp."

"Angie isn't at basketball camp," Miss Josie said, referring to his next-door neighbor and friend, who was also the best basketball player in their elementary school.

"She's going to summer school in the mornings. Something about an advanced math extra-credit course." Oliver shuddered.

"I'm sure your mom would love it if you cleaned your room," Miss Josie suggested.

"I cleaned it last month," Oliver said.

"You could read."

"Uncle Arthur forgot to bring books the last time he came to visit."

Miss Josie tsked sympathetically. She knew how much Oliver depended on his monthly book delivery from his uncle, who provided him with every story a kid could wish for.

Mr. Beiderman got up from his chair. "I've got to check on Princess Cutie. Sometimes she scales the curtains and can't get down." Princess Cutie was Mr. Beiderman's cat, which Hyacinth had given him and Laney had named. Mr. Beiderman walked to the door.

"I can teach you how to knit," Hyacinth offered her brother, holding her knitted rope in the air.

"If I ever take up knitting, feel free to stab me in the heart," Oliver replied.

"You can push me and Paganini on the tire swing," Laney suggested, her eyes brightening.

Oliver yawned. "It's too hot."

"Isa would do it," Laney grumbled.

Miss Josie tapped her chin with a finger. "Ooh, I know!"

"You're not going to talk about us making that disgusting piece of land next to the church into a garden again, are you?" Oliver said at the same time Miss Josie exclaimed, "You can make that unused land next to the church into a garden!"

Miss Josie's recommendation was met with collective boos.

"That place is haunted," Laney said. "Isa said so."

Hyacinth nodded. "I don't like walking past it. Isa said the vines that wrap around the gate reach out and grab people when they walk by."

"It's *not* haunted!" Jessie called out. "It has never been scientifically proven that ghosts actually exist."

"How do you know?" Oliver countered. "Have you studied them?"

"Think how nice it would be to have a place to rest in the middle of a hot day," Miss Josie continued. "People could get into the dirt and even plant vegetables! I'm sure Triple J would approve." Triple J was the church's pastor.

"Do you miss working at the botanical garden, Miss Josie?" Jessie asked, pushing aside the ivy so she could look inside. Miss Josie had been an educator at the New York Botanical Garden in the Bronx.

"I do miss it," Miss Josie replied. "I worked there for forty-five years. That's how I met Mr. Jeet. He was a groundskeeper, and he seemed to show up wherever I was. The rest is history." She smiled in Mr. Jeet's direction. Mr. Jeet was letting Hyacinth give him one pill at a time; he was slowly swallowing them with water and grimacing after each one. He sure had to take a lot of pills.

"If you had a garden, you could plant delicious things for Paganini to eat," Miss Josie suggested to Laney.

"Ooh, he would *love* that!" Laney replied. Paganini's

ears twitched at the sound of his name; then he jumped into a ceramic pot that held a ficus tree. Miss Josie gently lifted him out before he kicked dirt all over the floor, then set him on Mr. Jeet's lap.

Mr. Jeet used his right hand (his left hand still had limited mobility after his stroke two years ago) to play with Paganini's ears. His words came out slowly. "You're—lucky—you're—cute." He leaned down while Paganini sat up, and they did a nose bump.

Oliver rested his head on the cool metal table. It felt good against his cheek. "A garden sounds like a lot of work."

"Herman Huxley," Jessie sang from the window. "You are *so* like him."

Oliver was tired of his sister and her stupid comments and her stupid phone. "Stop saying that! You don't know anything!"

"Don't be mean to me because you're jealous of my phone," Jessie shot back, climbing through the window.

"Okay, kids," Miss Josie interjected. "Why don't I put out some tea and cookies—"

But Oliver didn't want tea and cookies. He wanted

the last word. "Why do you need a phone, anyways? It's not like you got into science camp and need to stay in contact with Mama and Papa. Isa is probably off having a great time without you, while you're stuck here all summer doing nothing."

"Oliver!" Mr. Jeet called out. Paganini leaped off his lap and onto the carpet, then scurried under an armchair. Mr. Jeet tried to get out of his chair, his face ashen and his arms shaking as he braced himself on the armrests. "Please—Oliver—no—fight—" But before he could finish his sentence, his knees buckled and he fell into Hyacinth.

"Miss Josie, help!" cried Hyacinth, struggling to support Mr. Jeet's weight.

"Jeet!" cried Miss Josie, running toward him.

Mr. Beiderman burst through the door just as Mr. Jeet crumpled to the floor. Hyacinth knocked the medicine cup over as she fell into the side table. The pills fell to the floor and scattered in every direction.

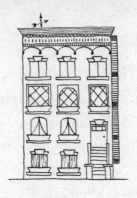

TWO

The next hour was a blur. Mr. Jeet didn't move, even when Miss Josie shook him and shouted into his ear. Jessie called 911. Oliver ran downstairs to their apartment to get Mama.

Mr. Beiderman put a blanket over Mr. Jeet's unmoving body, and Jessie couldn't help thinking that it was just like in the movies. Didn't they always put a blanket over dead bodies in movies? Her body felt brittle and bitterly cold, but she made herself go through the motions of helping.

She ushered Hyacinth, Laney, Paganini, and Franz into Miss Josie and Mr. Jeet's bedroom. Her sisters threw themselves into her lap and cried into her T-shirt while they waited for the ambulance. Jessie, who was used to letting Isa fill the role of primary comforter, patted her sisters awkwardly on their backs and found herself murmuring "It'll be okay" and "Don't worry; the doctors will know how to help him" and other things she didn't know were true.

At the sound of the ambulance sirens down the street, she heard Oliver leap down the stairs two at a time and then the building door bang open. The brownstone groaned under the hurried footsteps of the paramedics.

"Is he dying?" sobbed Laney while Paganini settled himself between Mr. Jeet's bedroom slippers.

"Of course not," Jessie said. But she didn't know.

They heard the paramedics rush through the door, then Miss Josie's wobbly voice as she answered questions about Mr. Jeet's age, health, and medicines.

"One . . . two . . . three," said a voice. Jessie disentangled herself from her sisters and opened the bedroom door a crack. The paramedics were lifting Mr. Jeet onto the stretcher. Laney crawled over and peeked out, then burst into fresh tears. Jessie closed the door and leaned against it. She listened to the paramedics talk to each other in low voices as they went down the stairs. Then she heard the brownstone door open and slam shut.

There was silence in the apartment.

Franz bayed, the deep, mournful sound cutting through the stillness of the room as they listened to the ambulance sirens fade into the distance.

❖ ❖ ❖

Oliver couldn't sleep. His clock read 11:03 p.m. His stomach felt funny, as if a restless octopus had taken up residence there. His brain was filled with the image of Mr. Jeet calling his name, clutching the right side of his body, then falling to the ground. His mom still hadn't come home from the hospital. That was a bad sign, right?

His clock clicked again: 11:04 p.m.

Mama had called only once, to say that the doctors were still doing tests but that Mr. Jeet was in good hands. Oliver didn't know what was taking so long. Mr. Beiderman—Oliver usually shortened his name to Mr. B for efficiency—had brought down SPAM sandwiches for dinner around six o'clock, when their father came home, but Papa and the kids had hardly touched them. Eventually Mr. B left, accusing the Vanderbeekers of "wasting perfectly good food."

11:05 p.m. The brownstone, usually filled with cheerful creaks, was ominously quiet. Oliver wished his bedroom window looked onto the street so he could see if Mama was coming home. Instead, his window looked across at the brownstone next door, where the neighbors kept their shades drawn all the time.

11:06 p.m. Still no sign of Mama.

Oliver jumped down from his loft bed and left his room. The kitchen and living areas were downstairs on the ground floor, while all the bedrooms were on the first floor, lined up so Jessie and Isa shared the bedroom facing 141st Street.

Oliver took a right down the hall and let himself into Jessie's room. His sister was snoring in her typical bulldozer way. He grabbed Isa's desk chair and rolled it to the window, then he perched on the edge of the chair and rested his elbows on the windowsill, looking for Mama's familiar straight black hair and her purposeful walk. He thought back to when he was little and used to watch out the window for Papa to come

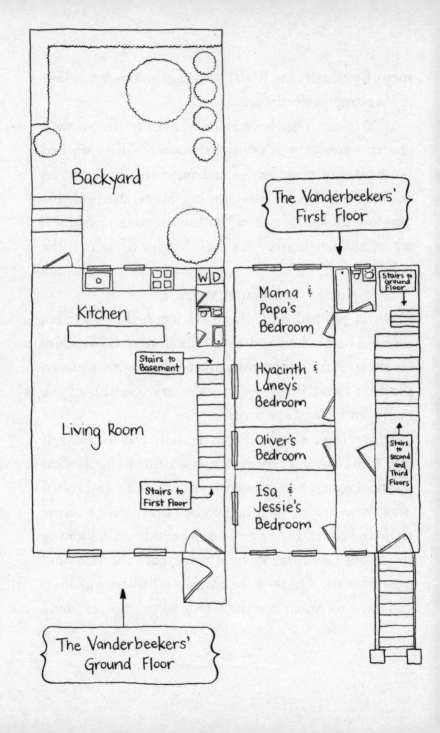

home from work, only Papa's hair was big and unruly and he walked as if he had all the time in the world. As members of a biracial family, the kids had inherited a surprising blend of physical characteristics from their parents. Although no one looked alike—the twins actually looked the most different from each other—there was a thread of resemblance that connected them and made them all uniquely Vanderbeeker.

The street outside was dark and quiet. It was the kind of dark and quiet where bad things could happen, things like words being said that could never be taken back or a neighbor dying in a hospital. Oliver sat there so long that the images of the street turned to a blur.

A rustle of bedsheets and a happy yelp from the other side of the room startled Oliver so much that the chair rolled out from underneath him and he crashed to the ground, his chin hitting the windowsill on the way down.

"Isa!" Jessie ran over to Oliver's crumpled body. Then, "Oh," she said, realizing her misidentification. Her voice turned flat. "It's you."

"Don't worry; I'm fine," Oliver retorted, rubbing his chin. "No need to help me up or anything."

"Okay," Jessie said before blinking three times and stumbling back to her bed.

"What happened?" Hyacinth asked as she and Laney burst into the room, with Franz skidding in behind them. "We heard a crash. Did someone get hurt?"

"Just me," Oliver called out from the spot by the window.

Laney skipped over. "What hurts? Do you want me to kiss it and make it feel better?"

"No," Oliver said.

Jessie sat up in her bed. She looked a lot more awake now. "Why is everyone in my room at eleven thirty-seven p.m.?"

Laney jumped onto Isa's bed and rolled around on the fluffy pillow pile. "I'm not tired," she announced. "I've been up for *hours*. How many dots are on a dice? Why do we call baby cats kittens? What makes a pig's tail curly?"

Oliver ignored her. "I'm waiting for Mama. She's not home yet."

Jessie glared at him. "I don't want you guys in here. I'm trying to sleep."

"But you have a window," Oliver protested.

"Nope," Jessie said, grabbing his shoulders and turning him around to face the door. She marched him out into the hallway, then did the same to Hyacinth. Laney was the only one left.

"Can I sleep in Isa's bed?" Laney asked, hugging Isa's one stuffed animal, a fuzzy wombat, close to her heart.

"Nope, nope, nope," Jessie replied. She removed the wombat from Laney's arms and threw it back on Isa's bed, picked her sister up, carried her out to the hall-way, and deposited her next to Oliver, Hyacinth, and Franz. Then the door closed firmly.

Hyacinth looked at Oliver. "Are you *sure* Mama's not home yet?"

"I've been waiting up for her. Papa went to bed an hour ago. I heard him talking to her on the phone. Mr. Jeet is staying in the hospital overnight." Oliver walked over to the top of the stairs that led down to the ground floor. He sat down on the top step. It had a perfect view of the front door. Laney, Hyacinth, and Franz squeezed onto the step on either side of him, and Oliver was comforted by the company. Tonight was one of those rare nights when he wished he shared a bedroom. He wanted the sounds of someone else in his room.

"Will Mr. Jeet be okay?" Hyacinth asked Oliver, leaning into him.

"Of course he'll be okay," Oliver said quickly. "Why wouldn't he?"

"He looked so sick," Hyacinth said, putting an arm around Franz and rubbing behind his ear.

The door to Jessie's room opened, and Jessie came out. "Now *I* can't sleep," she grumbled. She nudged Laney's hip with her foot. "Move over."

Three

Laney snuggled closer to Oliver on the step, and Jessie squeezed in between Laney and the handrail. George Washington emerged from the living room and leaped up the stairs, curling his big cat body at Oliver's feet.

"So I've been thinking," Jessie started at the same time Oliver said, "Do you think—"

"You go first," Jessie and Oliver said in unison.

Oliver suddenly felt silly. "It's stupid. Just an idea I had."

"There's no such thing as a dumb idea." Hyacinth said the phrase exactly the way Miss Josie did.

Oliver rubbed his eyes. "I don't know . . . I was just

thinking about what Miss Josie said earlier. Maybe we should, I don't know, do that thing she suggested?"

There was a long silence.

"Are you talking about cleaning your room?" Jessie ventured.

"No, listen," Oliver said, his words coming out in a jumble. "A garden. That's what we can do for Miss Josie and Mr. Jeet. Miss Josie never asks for anything, but she's been hinting about that garden for years. And I know Mr. Jeet misses being outside and seeing his friends. It's the perfect thing for us to have ready for him when he gets back from the hospital." Oliver didn't mention the fear that lodged itself in his brain, the one that said *if he gets back from the hospital.*

Oliver waited for his sisters to tell him how brilliant his idea was.

Hyacinth's eyes grew round. "I'm not going near that haunted place."

"Me neither," Laney commented. She looked out the darkened windows and shivered. "Plus there's a sign that says No Pass on there. That means if you pass the gate, you'll turn into a gremlin."

Oliver rolled his eyes. "I've never seen a sign there. Anyway, you can't even read."

"I can too!" Laney said. "That's what it says!"

Jessie spoke up. "That gate is locked up tight. I doubt the church will let us in. Who knows what's inside?"

"Miss Josie can help us convince them. She's been going to that church for a hundred years," Oliver said, undeterred.

"A hundred years?" Hyacinth exclaimed.

"He's exaggerating," Jessie told her. "But she *has* been going there for a long time."

"If we start working on it right away," Oliver continued, "we can have a big garden *extravaganza*." Oliver loved saying the word *extravaganza*. It was the same word the library used for its annual used-book sale, and rolling the word on his tongue never failed to thrill him. "We can do it in a couple of weeks, the day after Isa gets home!"

Jessie was still skeptical. "That's only eighteen days away. Plus, we don't know anything about gardens."

"Mama read *The Secret Garden* to us," Oliver said. "Gardening doesn't sound so hard. Anyways, you're the science person. A garden is a perfect place to do scientific experimentation, right?"

"That would be botany, which is not one of my scientific interests," Jessie pointed out.

"C'mon, Jessie. Do it for Mr. Jeet and Miss Josie." Then Oliver played his ace: "Stop acting like Herman Huxley."

"Herman Huxley!" Jessie exclaimed. Her voice lowered. "How dare you."

Oliver bit back a smile. "So? Are we muskrats or men? Wingbats or women? Ravenclaws or Hufflepuffs? Are we doing this or not?"

Jessie sighed. "You know, that did not even make any sense. But fine. I'll do it, but only because I love Miss Josie and Mr. Jeet."

Oliver looked at Hyacinth and Laney, who looked as if they'd rather face Voldemort than venture into the haunted garden. "So we're doing this?"

"Nope, never, no way," Hyacinth said, burying her face in Franz's neck.

Oliver sighed, then looked at Laney. "C'mon, Laney. We'll have so much fun. We can be just like Mary and

Dickon and Colin in *The Secret Garden*—you love that book. And think of a garden full of fresh food for Paganini!"

Laney shook her head, her pigtails bouncing across her face. "Paganini doesn't like gremlins either."

❀ ❀ ❀

It wasn't long before Laney and Hyacinth fell fast asleep, their heads nestled in Jessie's and Oliver's laps. After a long period of silence, Oliver sighed three times in a row, glancing at Jessie each time.

Jessie looked at him. "What's wrong with you?"

Oliver hesitated. "I feel bad about what I said to you today," he finally said.

Jessie was surprised. Her brother rarely apologized for anything.

Oliver grimaced. "You know, that thing I said? About Isa having a great time this summer without you?"

Jessie raised her eyebrows. "Oh, that."

"Well, I'm sorry, okay? That wasn't very nice of me."

Jessie's mind immediately rewound to April. She

remembered sitting around the dinner table while Isa shared the good news about getting accepted to orchestra camp with a full-tuition scholarship. She had waved the acceptance letter in the air and bounced excitedly on her feet, actions that were very out of character for reserved Isa. Mama and Papa were quiet as they reviewed the rest of the paperwork, and Jessie remembered glancing at the bill over their shoulders and seeing that the tuition was paid for but the room and board was not. A week later, Mama had picked up a part-time night job doing some accounting work for the local coffee shop.

She looked at Oliver. "I'm sorry I compared you to Herman Huxley."

Oliver shrugged. "It's okay."

They sat in silence for a long time before Mama returned. She looked as exhausted as Jessie had ever seen her. Her clothes were wrinkled, there was a coffee stain on her shirt, and dark circles hung underneath her eyes. Mama glanced up the stairs and smiled wearily at her kids in pajamas all squeezed together on the top step with Franz and George Washington.

"He's doing fine," Mama said quietly before anyone could say anything. She made her way up the stairs and kissed each of her kids on the cheek. "The doctors are doing a lot of tests. Miss Josie is staying with him tonight. The nurse set up a cot in Mr. Jeet's room for her."

"What happened?" Oliver whispered.

Mama sat on the next stair down, beside a purring George Washington. "He had another stroke."

"Is it affecting his left side again?" Jessie asked.

"Yes. There was a blood clot that led to a vessel in his brain, which is why he got dizzy and fell. He isn't talking yet. But he had medical help right away, so that's really good."

"What caused it?" Oliver asked. His voice had none of the confident swagger Jessie was used to hearing from her brother.

"Oh, lots of things," Mama said. "He was already at high risk because of his previous stroke. Once he's out of the hospital, we need to help him get lots of exercise and healthy food, like vegetables and fresh greens. He's a little *too* fond of Miss Josie's fried chicken. I should probably stop bringing him so many cookies."

Mama did not look pleased about that development. She believed it was her job to supply everyone in the neighborhood with cookies.

"When does he come back home?" Jessie asked.

"The doctor wants Mr. Jeet to have three really good days in a row before he'll get released. He'll also need to do physical therapy at the hospital."

Oliver moved Hyacinth's head off his lap and leaned her up against Laney. Jessie watched him get up, edge past Mama and George Washington, and go down the stairs to where a large picture frame hung by the front door. The area inside the frame was painted with chalkboard paint. The Vanderbeekers used it to write reminders and draw pictures. Under the area where Laney had drawn Paganini, Oliver made a chart.

When he returned to the top of the stairs, he sat in his original spot and fiddled with the hem of his pajama leg. "How is Miss Josie?"

Mama smiled wearily. "She's okay. I tried to get her to come home to sleep, but she's not budging from his side."

"Can we call her?" Jessie asked.

"Maybe tomorrow," Mama answered. "We'll see."

A door opened down the hallway, and Papa emerged from the darkness in his gray sweatpants and an old college T-shirt full of holes.

"Why is everyone on the steps?" he asked, squinting.

Mama stood up. "They were waiting up for me. We're going to bed." She picked up a sleeping Laney and went down the hall. "Can you grab Hyacinth?" she asked Papa.

His grizzly chin brushed against Jessie's cheek as he leaned over to pick Hyacinth up. "Go to bed now," he told Oliver and Jessie, then disappeared into Laney and Hyacinth's room behind Mama.

Jessie's body was stiff from sitting on the hard step for so long. She stood up and walked to her bedroom, already looking forward to sinking into her bed. Before she closed the door, she looked back down the hallway and saw her brother's silhouette. The headlamps of a car going down 141st Street flashed against the walls of the ground floor, and for one split second Jessie could see her brother's face. He looked wide awake, as if he planned to stay on that top step for a very, very long time.

WEDNESDAY, JUNE 27

Days Mr. Jeet in Hospital: 2

Days Until Garden
Extravaganza: 17

Four

ISA: Why didn't you tell me Mr. Jeet was sick?

JESSIE: Who told you?!?

ISA: I'm coming home right now.

JESSIE: Oh no, you are not. You need to stay right where you are. He's fine.

ISA: Laney told me that he's in the hospital! Is he dying?

JESSIE: He's NOT dying! Do not leave Ferris Lake! It will make him feel worse if you leave now.

Pause

ISA: Fine. I won't come back. But PROMISE to keep me updated.

JESSIE: I promise.

ISA: Say this out loud: I promise to keep Isa updated daily about anything that happens at the brownstone on 141st Street.

Pause

JESSIE: Okay, I said it. Happy?

ISA: Yes.

✵　✵　✵

Laney was lying on the fluffy rug in the basement, and Mr. Beiderman was *supposed* to be giving her a drawing lesson, but instead he was on his phone, talking to someone about saving a building from being torn down. Princess Cutie rested around his neck like a scarf.

"It has architectural significance," Mr. Beiderman was saying into the phone, "as well as historical importance. You don't want to get into another situation like the Dakota Stables. I know you've never forgiven yourself for that."

When he hung up, Laney had *lots* of questions. "Who were you talking to? What were you talking about? What are the Dakota Stables?"

Mr. Beiderman reached up to stroke Princess Cutie's forehead. "That was an old college friend of mine. She works at the Landmarks Preservation Commission, and she was asking my opinion about a building that's being considered for landmark status. When a building gets landmark status, that means it can't be changed without approval. It also means it can't be torn down."

"What about the stables?" Laney asked.

"The Dakota Stables used to be on Seventy-Fifth Street and Amsterdam, but it was made into a parking garage when horses stopped being the main form of transportation. It was being considered for landmark status when the garage tore down all the historical elements that made it special, so it was no longer worth considering for architectural significance." He pulled up an old stable photo on his phone and showed it to Laney.

"I wish there were still horses," Laney said. "That's sad about the building. It's really pretty."

Oliver ran down the basement stairs. "Laney! Why are you still in your pajamas? We've got to get over to the church!"

Laney looked up at her brother as she bit into a green breakfast cookie her mom had given her. Mama had experimented with adding spinach to her cookies this morning, and Laney had collected a whole *pile* of them. Each one of her siblings had given her theirs, which had never happened before. Laney loved green things: shamrocks, those lamb's ear plants that were as soft as Paganini's nose, and green M&M's, which Papa insisted were lucky. Laney had been saving green M&M's in a small jar since school had ended last week; she was very good at persuading her family to give the green ones to her.

Jessie came down the stairs behind Oliver. "I think we should wait until ten o'clock."

"I'm not going," Laney announced. "I don't wanna be turned into a gremlin."

Papa had just read Laney a book called *The Gremlins* by Roald Dahl. Gremlins were little, about as tall as Paganini when he stood up on his hind legs, and had horns coming out of their heads. They were known to be Up To No Good, and Laney did *not* want to meet one.

"You're *not* going to be turned into a gremlin," Oliver said impatiently. He was tugging at his hair; Laney knew he did that when he was stressed. He had yanked out a whole hunk of hair once when Mama accidentally washed his favorite white basketball jersey with Laney's flamingo Halloween costume and turned the jersey bright pink.

Hyacinth came down the stairs next, trailing a rope of yarn behind her. "I'm not going either. I don't want those vines to grab me."

"The garden is not haunted!" Oliver shouted. Then he took a deep breath and looked at his watch again. "The church should be open *now*, right?"

Mr. Beiderman interjected. "Why is it so important to get there early?"

"You know how Miss Josie always talks about making that empty land next to the church into a garden?" Oliver said. "It's been abandoned for years, so we thought we'd try to do something to it. We just need their permission."

Mr. Beiderman's face paled, and he abruptly stood up, turned away from the kids, and stomped up the stairs, disappearing from sight.

"Mr. Beiderman!" Laney called out. "I thought you were going to give me a drawing lesson!"

The Vanderbeekers looked at one another.

"His face looked like Mama's when she sees a mouse," Laney reported.

At the sound of the word "mouse," Franz pricked up his ears.

Jessie sighed and glared at Hyacinth. "Are you feeding the mice down here again?"

Hyacinth looked down and focused her attention on finger knitting.

"Is Mr. Beiderman afraid of mice?" Laney could not imagine anyone being afraid of mice. They had such cute noses and whiskers!

"Maybe he's feeling sad about his family," Hyacinth said. "You know how he gets sometimes."

Laney thought about this. Mr. Beiderman didn't really talk about his family much. Laney knew that his daughter, Luciana, had died six years ago, at age sixteen, along with Mr. Beiderman's wife, when a taxi had hit them as they were crossing the street. Isa had told Laney that the deaths of his wife and daughter were what had made Mr. Beiderman shut himself inside his apartment for so many years.

Sometimes Mr. Beiderman got so sad that he stopped

coming down for dinners and didn't answer his phone, even when Laney dialed his number five times in a row and left "I love you" messages each time. Mama said that he needed to be alone, but Laney always felt like crying when he shut himself inside his apartment for days at a time. She loved when he joined them for dinners or came downstairs in the evening to read her a bedtime story.

When Mr. Beiderman acted like this, Laney wanted to do something for him. When she fell down, her parents and sisters kissed whatever body part was hurting. Laney put her hand over her heart and felt it beat out a rhythm against her palm. What could she do to make Mr. Beiderman's heart feel better?

❧ ❧ ❧

After Laney had changed out of her pajamas, the Vanderbeeker siblings filed outside and headed west toward the church. There was silence as they walked past the row of brownstones on 141st Street. Jessie always felt a little in awe walking down their block. She liked to imagine the people who had built the brownstones from the ground up over a hundred years ago, and then all the people who had lived there since. Her next-door neighbors had cool jobs: one was a physical therapist who worked with dancers on Broadway; one was a custodian at the local high school; one was in construction, working on one of the huge office buildings going up on 55th Street and Third Avenue; and another worked as an educator at the Bronx Zoo. In the evenings, she would hear them coming home, along with laughter spilling out through the windows and music drifting from radios propped up on the windowsills as people prepared dinner or washed dishes.

At the end of the block, the gray stone church stood proudly with gleaming stained-glass windows and one impressive spire that rose above the height of the brownstones. Right before the church was a patch of weedy land surrounded by a chainlink fence covered in thick ivy, with a sign that could barely be seen through the overgrowth.

"See!" Laney said, standing on tiptoe and pointing at the sign. "It says No Pass."

Laney's siblings glanced at one another. Could Laney read?

"And that's why you get turned into a gremlin if you pass the gate," Laney concluded.

Oliver eyed her. "Where did you get that gremlin idea?"

Laney squished up her face. "I just *know.*"

Jessie poked her finger through the thick ivy, trying to look beyond it. The land used to be a play area for kids who went to the church's nursery school, but when the school closed down ten years before, there was no one to maintain and use the space on a regular basis. The church had closed off access to it; now the lot was the one neglected area on the block.

"Are you sure you want to do that?" Hyacinth took a big step away from the fence.

"I wonder if there's a way to get inside," Jessie said. "Like a gate or a door." She scanned the fence, looking for an opening.

Oliver tried to pull at some of the tangled vines, with little success.

"Man, this ivy is really tough—ARGHHHH! MY ARM!" Oliver started thrashing against the fence, trying to free himself.

Hyacinth and Laney screamed and started grabbing Oliver's other arm, trying to pull him from the fence, where a gremlin was undoubtedly snacking on his fingers. Jessie jumped in, yanking Oliver so hard that they all tumbled to the sidewalk in a big heap.

Then Oliver started laughing. His eyes teared up and he blurted out, "Fooled you!"

His sisters glared at him, but Oliver was cackling so hard, he didn't notice.

Jessie stood up and held out a hand to her sisters. Laney pointed at her elbow, and Jessie brushed off the gravel and gave it a kiss.

"Come on," Jessie said, glaring at Oliver. "Let's go visit Triple J."

Hyacinth glanced at her brother, who was lying on

the sidewalk, still laughing. "What about Oliver?" she asked Jessie.

Jessie rolled her eyes and said, "Leave him there," then started walking toward the church.

The pastor, a man named James Joseph Jackson who went by the nickname Triple J, had led the church for more than forty years. He was known throughout the neighborhood as wise and sensible, and even people who didn't go to his church found themselves stopping by to chat with him during the week.

Jessie, Hyacinth, and Laney walked up to the church and knocked on the solid wood door. When there was no answer, Jessie knocked again just as Oliver rejoined them. Still no answer, so all four kids pounded together. Triple J's office was far from the church door; plus he sometimes took out his hearing aids when he worked.

Their diligence was rewarded when the heavy door slowly opened and a cheerful voice greeted them in a big baritone. "Hello, my dear Vanderbeekers. Are you having a blessed day?"

Five

Triple J wore round eyeglasses and a white T-shirt with drawings of animals that kids from the Sunday school had made for him a few months ago when they'd been studying Noah's Ark. He was followed by a short, balding man whose baggy brown suit pants pooled around pointy brown shoes that looked as if they squeezed his toes.

"How is everyone today?" he asked, passing around fist bumps. "Have you met Mr. Huxley? We were having a budget meeting, so I'm especially glad you interrupted me." He winked at the kids.

Huxley? Oliver glanced at Jessie.

Mr. Huxley gave a bland wave.

"Are you Herman's dad?" Oliver asked.

"Yes," Mr. Huxley said.

"We're in the same class," Oliver told him.

"Uh-huh," he replied. Then he pulled out his phone and started typing away on it.

"Any word from Isa?" Triple J asked. "How does she like orchestra camp?"

"She's having a great time without us," Jessie told him, frowning. She handed him her cell phone. "Want to text her?"

Triple J took the phone, switched to his reading glasses, then pounded on the keys with his thumbs, dictating the message as he typed: "Hi there! Triple J here. Say your prayers. Eat vegetables. Tell your parents you love them." He pressed send and handed the phone back to Jessie. It buzzed almost instantly. Jessie glanced at the screen, then held it up to Triple J. Isa had already replied. "Triple J! Thanks for writing! I miss you!"

"Jessie texts Isa a billion times a day," Oliver informed Triple J.

"Sisters are the greatest gift," Triple J said amiably.

He ignored Oliver, who mumbled, "Ha!" under his breath. "What brings you kids by the church today? Am I lucky enough that you came just to visit me?"

"Actually, we *did* come to see you," Oliver said. "We have a proposition."

"That means it's a really great idea," Laney chimed in.

Triple J nodded, encouraging them to continue.

Oliver took a deep breath. "See, we were thinking of doing something here." He pointed toward the neglected lot next door. "We wanted to make it into a garden." Oliver caught the skeptical look on Mr. Huxley's face. "Or something."

Triple J's phone pinged, and he took it out of his pocket and squinted at the screen.

"Are you saying you want to play in there?" Mr. Huxley gestured dubiously at the trashed lot. "Wouldn't the park be better?"

"It wouldn't be for playing in," Jessie clarified. "We want to clean it up and make it into something everyone can enjoy."

Triple J said, "Mmm-hmm. That's a nice idea, nice idea." Then his phone pinged again, and he said, "Hold on." He answered, then said, "Is everything okay?"

into the phone. He gave an apologetic wave to the kids and whispered, "Mr. Huxley can help you," before stepping back into the church and leaving them with Mr. Huxley, whose attention was already back on his phone.

"So, can we do this?" Oliver asked him.

Mr. Huxley dragged his eyes off his phone. "Do what?"

"Use the lot next door," Jessie said.

"Wait a second," Mr. Huxley said with a pinched look on his face. "As far as I know, there isn't even a way to get inside that lot. Even if we could, I wouldn't give you kids a big piece of land to play around in. Think about the liabilities. What if you get hurt? The church can't afford a new boiler, let alone a lawsuit."

"But Triple J just said we could use it," Oliver said, fudging the truth, since Triple J *had* seemed a little distracted. "We could sign a release—you know, like the ones they give us at school when we go on field trips."

"Yeah," Jessie chimed in. She had brought home so many of those field-trip permission slips that she had memorized the language. "I'm happy to type out a release form and have us all sign it in triplicate."

Mr. Huxley shook his head, and his phone buzzed. Apparently something urgent had come up, because he said, "Triple J and I have a lot of budget items to discuss," before turning around and going back into the church.

Oliver yelled at Mr. Huxley's retreating figure. "But what about our garden idea?"

The answer was the church door closing in their faces.

The Vanderbeekers stared at the door.

"Now what?" Oliver asked.

* * *

The Vanderbeekers figured they needed to wait until Mr. Huxley left the building before they asked Triple J about the lot again. Mr. Huxley was such a downer.

Hyacinth watched Jessie and Oliver pace back and forth in front of the fence while she and Laney sat on the stoop of the neighboring brownstone, a respectable distance away from potentially grabby gremlin hands. Laney was lining up pebbles along the edges of the steps.

Under her breath, Hyacinth sang the introduction to "Come Sail Away," a song she had learned in chorus at school. From inside the lot, branches of a large tree hung over the fence, creating shade on the sidewalk. Hyacinth finished singing the last line of the second verse, *But we'll try best that we can to carry on,* and she couldn't help but think the branches were swaying exactly to the rhythm of her song.

Hyacinth took a pause before the chorus, and the branches stilled, as if waiting for her to continue. When she began again, the leaves rustled in delight and the branches stirred once more. She jumped off the steps and walked toward the fence, all thoughts of gremlins and grabby vines and haunted gardens gone from her mind. One of the tree branches arching over the fence danced in front of Hyacinth. When she reached out to graze it with her finger, a gentle summer breeze blew down the street, rustling the ivy. A glint of gold sparkled in the sunshine among the dark green leaves.

Hyacinth brushed the ivy aside. Nestled inside a tangle of vines was a brass lock.

Six

One of the last technology classes Oliver had taken before school ended was about how to create secure passwords. His teacher, Ms. Okeke, spoke about the importance of creating strong passwords so hackers couldn't steal your personal information or read your emails. Oliver and his best friend, Jimmy L, couldn't imagine anyone wanting to read their emails, which were mostly filled with homework questions or basketball stats and links to YouTube videos, but they did enjoy trying to create complicated passwords that they could never remember, using random combinations of the symbols above the number keys.

So when Hyacinth showed everyone her find, the

four-digit brass combination lock, Oliver knew just what to do. He thought about Ms. Okeke's list of passwords *not* to use because they were too common, and started with those numbers right away. Surely the person who had locked the land up tight ten years ago wouldn't have bothered much about lock security. Ten years ago was before he was born! Did they even have computers back then? Starting with 1-1-1-1, Oliver cycled through 2-2-2-2, then 3-3-3-3, and then all the same digits up to nine with no success.

"My confidence in you is fading," Jessie said as she watched over his shoulder.

"Stop hovering," Oliver muttered.

Next door, they heard the telltale creak of the wooden church door opening.

"Oliver," Hyacinth said uneasily, looking past him.

Oliver glanced over his shoulder to see Triple J emerge with a suitcase, Mr. Huxley right behind him. They faced the street, but a turn of the head would put the Vanderbeekers right in Mr. Huxley's sight line, and they did *not* want Mr. Huxley knowing what they were up to. Oliver frantically tried his next combination idea. At least Laney was unusually still; she was crouched down on the sidewalk, observing ants carrying a piece of apple to their colony.

"Maybe we should go," Jessie whispered.

Oliver felt a slight click as the numbers rolled into place and the lock disengaged. He slipped the lock off the latch and pushed the gate open. "C'mon!"

"Hurry!" Jessie whispered as a taxi rolled up in front of the church and Triple J walked toward it with his suitcase, Mr. Huxley still following.

Oliver slipped inside and turned to grab Laney and Hyacinth to yank them in, hoping their voices were muffled by the car engine running. Jessie entered last, pulling the gate closed behind her.

They heard a car vroom off down the street, and then Mr. Huxley's toe-pinching shoes tapping a staccato rhythm against the sidewalk toward them. He stopped almost directly in front of the gate; the kids could hear his coarse breathing on the other side of the ivy-covered fence. Oliver's heart was beating so loudly that the thump echoed in his ears. Laney had buried her head in Jessie's chest, and Hyacinth had nestled into Oliver's side. The sound of a garbage truck on the avenue covered Laney's whimpers.

After what seemed like hours, Mr. Huxley marched away from the lot, his steps accompanied by what sounded like happy humming. They listened until his footsteps faded away.

Then the Vanderbeekers slowly turned around to take their first look at the lot.

✸ ✸ ✸

"Ew," Oliver said, his face wrinkling in distaste. "Is that a toilet over there?"

Jessie followed Oliver's finger to where there was indeed a toilet.

"Maybe the gremlins live in there," Laney said uneasily.

"In the toilet?" Oliver was skeptical.

"There's a bathtub too," Hyacinth said, pointing.

Jessie didn't respond. Her eyes scanned the land past trash and weeds and neglect. There was a tree next to the fence with sprawling, begging-to-be-climbed branches, and near the back of the lot was another tree with a vinelike trunk that had woven itself through the fence, reaching for the sky. Ivy covered the fences and boxed in the lot on all four sides, scrabbling up the sides of the church buildings and serving as a barrier to busy city sounds. A host of sparrows must have been tucked into the branches of the tree, because chirps filled the air, as if the birds were having a disco party. The lot was beautiful and wild but also very neglected.

The sight reminded her of a hike in the Palisades she had taken with her family the year before. They had spent a glorious day wandering beneath majestic trees, slipping off their shoes and stepping into icy streams, and venturing through overgrown vine- and moss-covered pathways.

Jessie glanced at her siblings. Hyacinth stood up against the fence, fumbling for the latch to the gate.

Oliver, however, was already trying to pull up some of the ivy and weeds from the ground so he could make a path to the bathtub.

Hyacinth stepped into the garden and tried to pull Oliver back. "Don't go any farther!"

"I'm trying to clear a path," Oliver said. He yanked at more weeds. "Ouch," he said, dropping a weed with skinny thorns along its stems.

"Be careful," Jessie cautioned.

Hyacinth grabbed her brother's hand and turned it over so she could examine the injury.

Jessie, seeing an opening for getting Hyacinth to embrace the garden, swooped in. "Wouldn't it be amazing to have a secret spot for Mr. Jeet and Miss Josie? Think of what we could do to this space."

Oliver, who understood Hyacinth best, clinched it. "It would be the best *present* for them, don't you think? Plus, it would be a huge *surprise*."

Jessie watched Hyacinth process the information. Giving surprise gifts was her weakness.

"I guess it wouldn't make sense for gremlins to be in a garden," Hyacinth finally said, looking up at the tree next to her. "In the Roald Dahl book, the gremlins were up in the sky dismantling the airplane, not on the ground."

"Exactly," Oliver said with a snap of his fingers. "What about you, Laney? This is pretty cool, right?"

Laney was searching through the dirt, looking for

rocks for her collection and utterly unconcerned about gremlins.

"We need gardening gloves," Hyacinth said, looking at Oliver's hands. "And gardening supplies, like a trowel and a rake. Mandy had a trowel."

"Who's Mandy?" Laney asked, instantly suspicious. She prided herself on knowing all her siblings' friends. "There's no Mandy in your class."

"No, Mandy from the book *Mandy*. She lives in an orphanage and climbs over a wall every day to walk to an abandoned cottage where she has her own garden." Hyacinth looked around at the tumble of vines and plants.

"We definitely need gardening supplies," Jessie said. "Who has allowance money? Ooh, Oliver, you're rolling in cash!"

Oliver frowned. "I've been saving for my bike."

"I can give all my money," Laney said. "I have forty-three dollars."

"Forty-three dollars!" Oliver exclaimed. "How?"

"I put them in my piggy bank," she said.

Hyacinth had only three dollars; she always spent her allowance at the arts and crafts store as soon as she got it. Jessie had seventeen dollars. The sisters looked at Oliver.

"I've plunged toilets to earn money for that bike," he informed them. "And I *still* need to earn another eighty dollars." Oliver did extra chores for Mr. Smiley, a building superintendent two doors down and Angie's father, to make money, like mopping, cleaning the windows, and the most abhorred task: plunging toilets, which got stopped up frequently in the prewar building.

"Oliver," Jessie said. "Laney just offered up her entire savings."

Oliver pressed his lips closed. "I'll pitch in fifteen dollars," he mumbled.

"Awesome." Jessie paused for a millisecond. "That will be seventy-eight dollars. Plenty of money."

The Vanderbeekers looked out at the land. Sure, there was the toilet and the bathtub and enough trash to fill an entire dumpster, but if they squinted really, really hard, they could see what this place could be: the garden of Miss Josie and Mr. Jeet's dreams.

Seven

Laney's mind was bursting with ideas for the garden. She couldn't wait to start!

"It's our secret project," Jessie and Oliver coached Laney as they walked back home to gather their money so they could head to the garden store.

"I know, I know," Laney said. She was super good at keeping secrets.

"Do you think it's okay if we go in there even though Mr. Huxley said not to?" Hyacinth asked.

"Of course," Jessie and Oliver said at once.

"Mr. Huxley never specifically said we couldn't use it," Jessie clarified. "He just said that thing about liability and not wanting the church to get sued."

Hyacinth did not look convinced.

"Look," Jessie said, "if it makes you feel better, I'll write up a liability release form when we get home."

They filed into the brownstone, and Franz was so elated to see Hyacinth that he knocked her down and slobbered all over her face. Mama was on the phone, pacing back and forth in the living room and saying things into the phone like "deductibles" and "ambulance costs" and "preexisting conditions." Laney followed her siblings upstairs to Jessie's bedroom, where Jessie kept her word. She wrote up the release, and everyone signed it.

We hereby release Triple J and his church and Mr. Huxley from all liability for any injuries sustained by said participants while gardening on Harlem Gospel Baptist Church land.
Date: June 27
Signed:
Jessie   Oliver   LANEY
Hyacinth

"Okay, that's done," Jessie said, carefully filing the piece of paper in her desk drawer. "Now there's no 'official' reason why we can't go in there."

"Shouldn't we check with Triple J one more time?" Hyacinth asked, rubbing Franz's ears.

Jessie sighed. She took out her phone and called the church. "Hello," she said. "I'm trying to find Triple J."

There was a pause; then Jessie said, "Oh no! I hope everything is okay! . . . No, it's not urgent. We'll see him when he gets back." She put down her phone. "Triple J's brother in South Carolina fell down the stairs, and Triple J is heading down there to take care of him. He could be gone for a month. And Ms. Sandra said she's off to Puerto Rico tomorrow with her family, so the office will be closed for two weeks." Ms. Sandra was the church's meticulous administrator.

"What is going on with all these injuries?" Oliver asked.

"What do you think, Hyacinth? Should I try his cell?" Jessie asked.

Hyacinth bit her lip, then said, "No, we shouldn't disturb him."

"Great!" Jessie said. "Now let's get the money we're pitching in and create a budget."

A few minutes later, a pile of crumpled bills and spare change littered Jessie's desk. She wrote the total amount on the front of the envelope. On the other side, she wrote down their ideas for what they needed in the garden.

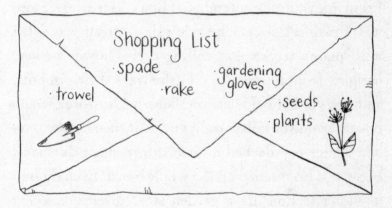

When they were done, Laney skipped down the stairs, kissed Paganini on the nose, kissed Mama on the nose (Mama was still on the phone, now talking about "out-of-network providers"), and avoided kissing George Washington, because he got grumpy when he was woken up from naps.

Mama gave Jessie money to get lunch at Castleman's, since she hadn't had time to go grocery shopping. Laney could not believe the luck of the day! A garden discovery, a shopping trip to the garden store, and now Castleman's!

✦ ✦ ✦

From May until September, Hiba's Hardware Store was a magical place. The sidewalk in front was filled with plants stacked on rolling carts, flower baskets hanging from the awnings, bushy trees sitting in pots, and trays of baby flowers on shelves. The store owners on either side of Hiba's didn't mind if the outdoor garden center encroached a bit on their sidewalk space, because it brightened up the whole block. Even though it wasn't technically a garden store, everyone knew what you were talking about if you referred to it that way.

Hyacinth was the first to reach Hiba's, which was just past Harlem Coffee, close to St. Nicholas Park. She went immediately to her favorite tree and wrapped her arms around it. The tree felt solid and comforting.

Hiba called it by the scientific name, *Tilia tomentosa*, which Hyacinth thought was a beautiful name. Hyacinth also gave the tree a nickname: Tilia of the Eternal Spring.

Today Tilia of the Eternal Spring looked happy and healthy. Hyacinth checked her leaves and examined her trunk. Then she closed her eyes and made a wish before turning the price tag over. It was still forty-five dollars, too expensive to buy for Mr. Jeet and Miss Josie's garden.

"One day," Hyacinth whispered into Tilia's leaves.

"Are you talking to the tree again?" Oliver asked before opening the door and stepping inside the store. The little bell hanging from the doorknob tinkled merrily.

Hyacinth gave her tree one more gentle squeeze before following her siblings inside.

Hiba's Hardware Store was narrow and very cramped. Items were stacked on top of one another or nestled into bins or containers. Customers weren't allowed past the counter at the front. Instead, you had to tell Hiba or whoever was working there what you needed and they would disappear into the depths of the store and retrieve it. Hyacinth thought this arrangement quite efficient.

"Hello, friends. What may I do for you today?" This was Hiba's customary greeting, and she said it from behind a tower of paint cans she was stacking on the display by the counter.

"We need some things," Jessie told her, handing her their list.

"So many people asking for gardening tools! I put everything there." She gestured to the wall behind the Vanderbeekers, the one area of the store that was easily accessible to customers, where hooks from floor to ceiling showcased a dizzying array of gardening items.

"I want this!" Laney said, reaching out to grab a red trowel. "And this!" She took a matching spade down.

"How are Miss Josie and Mr. Jeet?" Hiba asked. "Usually by this time of year, they've come in to see me to buy soil or pots."

The Vanderbeekers exchanged glances.

"Mr. Jeet had another stroke yesterday," Jessie told her. "He's in the hospital."

Tears filled Hiba's eyes. "I'm so sorry to hear that. I will be holding them in my heart." She bowed her head and touched her heart with both hands.

"We want to make a beautiful garden for them—" Laney began.

"—in our backyard, of course," Oliver finished.

Hiba nodded. "You browse around, and let me know if I can help you with anything."

The Vanderbeekers' stomachs were grumbling for lunch by the time they had made their choices. They took four trowels and four little rakes for churning up the dirt. They ogled the gardening gloves—some of the fancier ones had sturdy black rubber grips—but they went with the cheaper cloth versions instead. Then there were a couple of watering cans for six dollars each, which they decided they needed even though they weren't on the list. The shovels and rakes were expensive—the cheapest ones started at twenty-five dollars—so the Vanderbeekers decided to quietly "borrow" Papa's when he wasn't using them.

Everything was a lot more expensive than they'd thought it would be.

"I guess we can't get the tree," Hyacinth said, staring longingly out the window at Tilia of the Eternal Spring.

SALES RECEIPT

Date: 6/27

Qty.	Description	Price	Amount
4	spades	$3	$12
4	trowels	$3	$12
4	gardening gloves	$3.50	$14
2	watering cans	$6	$12
		Subtotal	$50
		Tax	$4.44
		Total	$54.44

Sale Made with:
[ ] Cash
[ ] Credit Card
[ ] Check, No. _____
[ ] Other

When their purchases were packed up and paid for, the Vanderbeekers stepped out of the store and onto the sidewalk. Hiba came out behind them.

"Please," she said before they headed off to get lunch. Hyacinth watched her pick up Tilia of the Eternal Spring and put it in front of her. "Please, for this garden you are making. I know you will take good care of her."

Hyacinth was speechless. An image of Tilia growing into a big and beautiful tree sprang into her mind. She could already imagine Mr. Jeet sitting on a bench underneath a grown-up Tilia, looking out at the garden with Franz by his side.

"Thank you," she whispered, touching Tilia's bright green leaves. "We can put her next to the Silver Queen."

"What's the Silver Queen?" Oliver asked.

"That big silver maple tree in the garden," Hyacinth said. "They can be friends."

Oliver shrugged and leaned down to wrap his arms around the tree pot to pick it up, grunting as he did so. "If I'm carrying this thing," he told Hyacinth, "you need to buy me at least three cheese croissants for lunch."

* * *

Oliver's arms ached from carrying Hyacinth's tree, which she insisted he refer to as Tilia of the Eternal Spring, a block away to Castleman's Bakery. This did not bode well for bringing Tilia to the garden, which was eight blocks away, nor was it a good sign for his atrophying arm muscles. He needed to do more push-ups to stay in shape or his friends would be worlds ahead of him when they returned from basketball camp.

When they got to Castleman's, Oliver set Tilia down with a groan on the sidewalk by the door. The Vanderbeekers stepped inside the blessedly air-conditioned bakery and breathed in the smell of cheese croissants and spicy apple turnovers.

"Hey, Vanderbeekers," Benjamin called out. Mrs. Castleman, Benjamin's mom, waved.

"Hey, Benjamin," they chorused. "Hi, Mrs. Castleman."

"Nice jersey," Oliver said. Benjamin always wore a football jersey under his apron.

"How is Isa doing?" Benjamin asked at the same time Jessie said, "Isa's fine; don't worry." Then they laughed, because even though Benjamin was friends with all the Vanderbeekers, he definitely preferred Isa to anyone else in the world, and had even taken her to his eighth-grade dance in January. Oliver couldn't understand what the point of the dance was—they just listened to music and danced? Why? But his whole family had made a big fuss about it as if it was really special.

Laney and Hyacinth made a beeline for the air-conditioner unit and stood in front of the vents to cool off. Jessie went to the display case to give their order to Mrs. Castleman, and Oliver collapsed into a chair by the front door and tried to shake some feeling into his arms.

Benjamin left the register and joined Oliver at the café table. "What's with the tree?" Benjamin asked.

"Not 'tree,'" Oliver said. "That, for your information, is Tilia of the Enduring Spring. Or is it Endearing Spring? I don't remember."

"Hyacinth is still obsessed with *Anne of Green Gables*, huh?" Benjamin observed.

"Yup." Auntie Harrigan had given Hyacinth the audiobook for her birthday back in February, and since then, Hyacinth had listened to it from beginning to end at least thirteen times and could recite full passages from it.

Outside, a thin woman wearing exercise gear stopped to examine the tree. Oliver, not wanting her to tamper with it, tapped the window. She looked up and made a gesture that translated into "Can I take this?" Oliver and Benjamin shook their heads, and they watched her walk off in disappointment.

"People are going to keep thinking it's free," Benjamin observed. And it was true, because usually anything left on the curb in the city was fair game for anyone who was willing to carry it home. That was how the Vanderbeekers had found the beautiful rugs that now covered the concrete floors of the brownstone basement. "Keep an eye on the tree. I'll be right back."

Benjamin jogged to the back room and returned a minute later with a bike lock.

Oliver gaped. "Are you going to lock up the tree?" When Benjamin grinned and went outside, Oliver followed. Benjamin wrapped the bike-lock cord around the tree and attached it to the metal rails of the bakery window boxes.

When Benjamin was done, they stepped back to admire the new tree security. Oliver was about to comment on Benjamin's great idea when he heard someone shout, "Watch out!" The screech of bike wheels filled his ears. Before he could register what was going on, Oliver found himself tumbling to the sidewalk. A second later, he heard someone say, "Are you okay?"

Oliver knew who it was without even looking up.

Eight

Jessie had been waiting for Mrs. Castleman to ring up their lunch items when she glanced out the window—just in time to see a bike knock her brother over. She flew out the door and kneeled down next to Oliver, who had a nasty skinned knee and a scraped elbow. Herman Huxley had abandoned his bike on the sidewalk and was hovering over Oliver.

"Are you okay?" he kept asking, again.

"You should watch where you're going," Benjamin told him.

"It was an accident!" Herman said.

"Ha," mumbled Oliver, blowing on his knee and trying to brush off the gravel around the broken skin.

Laney, Hyacinth, and Mrs. Castleman had now joined them and were clucking over his injuries.

"Do you need an ambulance?" Laney asked.

"It was an accident," Herman repeated. When no one acknowledged him, he picked up his bike. Jessie froze when she saw what Herman was riding.

The bike was the exact same one Oliver had been saving up for since January, and every Vanderbeeker knew that because it was all Oliver had talked about for months. A picture of the bike printed from the Internet was taped to his bedroom door, complete with a graph that showed how close he was to saving up for it.

❊ ❊ ❊

Oliver fumed. Herman didn't have just any old mountain bike. It was the Eastern Racer 500, black with a blue racing stripe, and Oliver had been plunging toilets, mopping floors, and cleaning windows to earn enough money for one. Not only was he working his fingers to the bone, but he was also penny-pinching as if he lived during the Great Depression. No churros from Manny the churro guy, no books from the library sale, and no new basketball sneakers, even though the treads on his pair were worn and slick. Despite all of this, Oliver was merely halfway to getting his Eastern Racer 500.

The fates were cruel indeed.

Oliver swallowed the jealousy creeping into his throat, but he couldn't force himself to accept Herman's apology. Seeing him made Oliver recall every single bad Herman memory from the past year: How Herman walked into school with the newest shiny smartphone or the latest special-edition sneaker. The lift tickets hooked to his coat zipper after winter break, from his trip to the Swiss Alps. The box of fancy chocolates he brought to school and *shared with no one.* Who did stuff like that?

Mrs. Castleman was digging through her first-aid kit for bandages big enough to cover Oliver's knee and elbow when Herman finally left. No one else really paid attention—they were too busy hovering over Oliver—but Oliver watched Herman turn a corner and disappear.

"There, all done," Mrs. Castleman said, packing up her first-aid kit. "Now let's get you some food."

Oliver's knee stung when he got up and limped back to the bakery, but a skinned knee couldn't keep him from cheese croissants. His sisters made him sit down while they helped Mrs. Castleman and Benjamin grab their pastries, lemonade, and fresh fruit. Benjamin pulled the top of his apron over his head and let it hang around his waist, the signal that he was off duty, and joined them for lunch around the café table by the front window. Hyacinth kept an eagle eye out for Tilia of the Eternal Spring, in case anyone dared to pick the bike lock and take off with her.

"What's the tree for?" Benjamin asked.

The Vanderbeekers filled him in on Mr. Jeet's health issues and how they wanted to create a garden for him to enjoy while he recovered.

"Are you going to visit him?" Benjamin asked. "Do you want to bring some pastries to the hospital?"

The Vanderbeekers didn't have to think twice about that offer.

The Vanderbeekers were quite a sight as they trooped from Castleman's Bakery to Harlem Hospital. They had loaded the tree onto an old hand truck Mrs. Castleman found in the bakery supply room, and Jessie was put in charge of wheeling Tilia of the Eternal Spring, while Oliver limped along next to her to make sure the tree didn't roll off. Laney carried the garden supplies, and Hyacinth transported the enormous box of pastries that Mrs. Castleman had put together and tied up with baker's twine.

Harlem Hospital was on Malcolm X Boulevard on the two blocks between 135th and 137th Streets, a ten-minute walk from Castleman's. When they arrived, they stepped into the big lobby and headed straight to the information desk.

"We're here to see Mr. Jeet," Jessie informed the woman at the desk from behind the tree.

The woman, who had a name tag that said Shanna, tapped on her computer with long, manicured nails. Hyacinth and Laney leaned around the counter to get a better look at them; Shanna's nails were painted a blue-black color and individually decorated with silver and gold stars.

"Your nails are very pretty," Laney noted. "Did your mommy paint them for you?"

Shanna laughed but didn't look away from her computer. "I got them done at the salon."

"Ooh," Laney said. "Fancy."

"I go to Dazzle Nails around the corner. Ask for Jupiter. Her nail art is *good.*"

Hyacinth and Laney filed that information in their heads to ask Mama about later.

"You visiting Charles Jeet?" Shanna asked, finally looking up at the kids.

The Vanderbeekers nodded.

"He's in Intensive Care on the sixth floor, but you can't go up without an adult. You got an adult with you?"

"Do I count as an adult?" Jessie asked, looking around the tree to see Shanna.

"How old are you?"

"Almost thirteen?"

"Then no."

Laney, who had guzzled two large cups of lemonade

at Castleman's Bakery, suddenly had to go to the bathroom. Immediately. She tugged on Jessie's sleeve. "Bathroom! I need to go now! It's an emergency!"

Shanna pointed a finger. "Bathrooms are down the hall to the right," she said. "Next!" she called to the line that had built up behind them.

"I want to visit him today," Oliver grumbled as they made their way down the hall. "That's a stinky rule."

"You guard the tree," Jessie instructed Oliver, leaving him outside the ladies' room with Tilia, the bakery box, and the bag of gardening supplies. She disappeared inside with Hyacinth and Laney.

His sisters took their sweet time in the bathroom, so Oliver had plenty of time to people-watch. He noticed the elevators were right next to the bathrooms, and he remembered that Shanna had said Mr. Jeet was on the sixth floor. It seemed a shame to come all this way and not even say hi to him. A quick visit couldn't hurt, right? They were kids, sure, but they were family. Mr. Jeet and Miss Josie would count as the adults once they got upstairs.

Oliver glanced back at the information desk, where Shanna was mobbed by a new group of people needing visitor passes. Then he rolled Tilia to a sunny window next to another plant so she could get some sun and have company. He returned to his spot by the bathrooms just as his sisters emerged.

"Where's Tilia of the Eternal Spring?" Hyacinth said immediately.

"She's hanging out by the window, soaking up the rays, living the good life," Oliver said. "Come on, let's go see Mr. Jeet."

Nine

Jessie wasn't so sure about breaking into the Intensive Care Unit, but Oliver gave a persuasive argument. They joined a herd of people entering the elevator, and no one seemed to care that four unaccompanied kids were wandering around. They made it to the sixth floor and exited with a couple who did not look one bit like them, but the Vanderbeeker kids were biracial anyway, so maybe the hospital staff would assume they were all together.

The kids trailed the couple, who weaved through the hallways as if they had navigated them before, and Jessie was glad to follow them, because the hospital was a maze! They were almost in the Intensive Care Unit—they had passed a sign with arrows pointing in the direction they were walking—when their luck ran out. The couple stepped into a patient's room, and the Vanderbeekers had no choice but to keep going. Jessie kept a lookout for a room with Mr. Jeet's name on it, but then they turned a corner and ran right into the nurses' station.

The Vanderbeekers hoped no one would notice them, but three nurses behind the counter raised their eyebrows and stood up at the same time.

"Where do you think you're goin'?" asked one, while another inquired, "Who are you with?" and the last one said, "Are you lost?" The nurses wore matching teal-blue scrubs, but their expressions ranged from unamused (the first nurse) to concerned (the second nurse) to pleasant (the third nurse).

"We're here to visit Mr. Jeet!" Laney said, smiling up at them. "We brought him treats from Castleman's Bakery."

The unamused nurse clicked her tongue. "This is an intensive care unit. Kids shouldn't be wanderin' around."

"He's family," Oliver said. "We have to see if he's okay."

"How are you related?" she said, eyeing Oliver's bandaged knee and elbow.

"We're neighbors," Jessie clarified. "But he's like a grandfather."

"*Like* a grandfather means he's not *actually* your grandfather," she replied, her voice sharp.

Laney pushed out her lip. "He belongs to us. We love him."

The third nurse, the pleasant one with eyes that were warm and happy, put a hand on the mean nurse's arm. "I got this," she said to her.

The mean nurse rolled her eyes, dropped into her office chair, and went back to her paperwork, muttering to herself.

The second nurse, the concerned one, wrinkled her brow. "He's not well enough for visitors right now. Maybe you can come back—with your parents—when he's moved out of the Intensive Care Unit."

Then the pleasant nurse said, "But it is so sweet of you to come and to bring food. I will definitely let him know you stopped by."

"Can we stick our head in and say hello? Just for a

second?" Jessie pleaded. "I think he would want to see us."

The conversation was getting to be too much for the unamused nurse, because she stood back up and swept her hands away from her, as if she was shooing the Vanderbeekers away. "Go on, we can't have you gettin' in the way while the doctors are workin'."

"I'm sorry," the pleasant nurse said. "I wish I could help you."

Laney beckoned her to lean closer. "Are you sure Mr. Jeet is okay?" she whispered.

"We're taking very good care of him," the nurse whispered back.

"You can have this whole box of pastries if you take extra, super-duper good care of him," Laney said, taking the box from Hyacinth and holding it up to the nice nurse.

"Well, isn't that sweet of you? We do love pastries, but we would take good care of him regardless."

"Can you make sure to give a couple to Miss Josie? That's Mr. Jeet's wife," Jessie said.

"I sure will," the nurse said, taking the box. "And

I'll let Josie know you came by. She's a real sweetheart."

"But don't give any to that lady," Laney said, pointing at the mean nurse, who was scowling at them.

The nice nurse winked at the kids, and the Vanderbeekers turned around to go back to the elevators. They followed the signs, but somehow they got turned around in the maze of hallways.

"I thought we went past here already," Oliver said. "We've seen that picture before." He pointed to a picture of a waterfall with the words "Believe in Yourself" written in curly script.

Jessie peered down the hall. "I think the elevators are that way," she said.

"Wait! Look!" Hyacinth said, pointing.

There, across the way, was a patient room with a card that said JEET stuck into a clear plastic holder.

The Vanderbeekers crept to the door and peeked in.

Mr. Jeet lay on a hospital bed, his eyes closed, surrounded by machines that were beeping and flashing. A bag of fluid hung from a rod, and the bottom had a long, clear tube that attached to his arm. His hospital gown hung loose over his shoulders, and his face was sunken and filled with wrinkles, like craters on the moon. He was very, very still.

Mama and Miss Josie were sitting on chairs across from Mr. Jeet. Miss Josie had her head on Mama's shoulders, and their bodies were hunched over, weighed down with grief.

The Vanderbeeker kids slowly backed away.

"He's really sick, isn't he?" Hyacinth whispered.

"I want to give him a hug," Laney said, tugging at Jessie's hand.

Jessie put her arms around Laney and squeezed her tight. "I think he needs rest, Laney Bean."

Oliver scrubbed the back of his hand over his eyes. Big tears rolled down Hyacinth's face.

They stood there, clumped together in the hallway, until a nurse rolling a gurney gave them a funny look as she passed by.

"We should go before we get in trouble," Jessie finally said. Her siblings nodded, then turned back down the hallway and found the elevators after paying extra-careful attention to the signs. They went back down to the ground floor, wheeled Tilia of the Eternal Spring out of the hospital, and walked all the way home in complete silence.

Ten

That night, Mama put together a gigantic salad for dinner. She was so distracted, she didn't even ask the kids about their day. Which was good, because they had done a lot of things they didn't really want to share with their parents.

"How's Mr. Jeet?" Hyacinth asked, even though she had already seen with her own eyes how he was doing. She plucked a piece of spinach from the salad bowl and offered it to Franz. He snatched it from her hand, chewed it for half a second, then spat it out on the floor in a slobbery green blob.

Mama pasted a big smile on her face. "Oh, he's doing fine. Just fine," she said as she shook up the salad dressing. "Put this on the table for me, sweetie."

Mr. Beiderman came clumping down the stairs with a stack of tins in his arms.

"I brought some food to share," he announced.

"You shouldn't have," Oliver muttered under his breath.

Mama's face hardened when she saw what Mr. Beiderman was holding. "Mr. Beiderman, you cannot keep eating that!" She grabbed the metal tins of SPAM and glared at the nutritional information. "Sixteen grams of fat in two ounces!" She tossed the tins into the trash as if they had said rude words to her.

Mr. Beiderman immediately went on the defensive. "I'm perfectly healthy."

"Ha!" Mama said. "You haven't seen your doctor in six years!" She grabbed the spare set of keys to Mr. Beiderman's apartment from a nail on the wall next to the laundry room and tossed it to Papa, who caught it cleanly in one hand.

"I'm on it!" Papa said, jogging up the stairs.

"Don't you dare get rid of my SPAM!" Mr. Beiderman yelled.

"Sorry! General's orders," Papa called out before the stairwell door closed.

Mama set out their largest serving bowl, filled with enough salad for a ravenous herbivorous dinosaur.

"Is that *all* we're eating?" Jessie asked, squinting at the salad.

"Of course not," Mama said. She put on an oven mitt and pulled a tray of baked chicken breasts from the oven. She slid the chicken onto a serving platter and handed it to Oliver, who staggered from the weight. Mama took the serving utensils and piled the salad and chicken on everyone's plate.

The kids pushed the salad around and occasionally passed greens under the table to Paganini, who hopped between them with glee.

Papa returned, a bulging bag of tinned meats in his arms. They clinked against one another when he walked down the stairs. "I think I got all of them!"

Mr. Beiderman scowled, but Hyacinth sensed that he was secretly pleased that someone cared enough about him to make sure he ate something that didn't come from a can.

After he stuffed the bag of forbidden food into the trash can, Papa sat down. His face fell when he saw the huge salad Mama had loaded onto his plate. He took the fork and bravely put a big bite into his mouth.

"When is Mr. Jeet coming home?" Hyacinth asked.

Mama choked on a piece of chicken she had just put into her mouth, then took her time swallowing a big gulp of water.

"Well . . ." she began. Everyone stopped eating and waited for her to respond. Laney passed Paganini a piece of arugula. "There are some . . . complications—"

"What complications?" Oliver demanded.

"Is he going to die?" Hyacinth asked.

"—so he's going to stay longer than we thought," Mama finished. She looked at Hyacinth. "Honey, he's not going to die! Don't cry. They want him really healthy and with a better range of movement before they release him. When he comes back, he'll have to go upstairs on his own, which won't be easy."

"He can stay in our apartment," Laney suggested.

"That's a great idea!" Hyacinth said. "He can stay in our room. I can bring him food."

"That still requires stairs," Oliver pointed out.

"But only one flight instead of two," Hyacinth countered.

Papa leaned over and kissed Hyacinth's cheek. "We'll see."

Hyacinth knew "We'll see" was really adult code for "No," but she wasn't ready to give up yet. Not if it meant Mr. Jeet and Miss Josie could come back home as soon as possible.

* * *

Jessie couldn't sleep. The image of Mr. Jeet lying in the hospital bed—so, so still—haunted her. She stared up at the ceiling, at the cracks that Isa said looked like Eastern Europe but Jessie thought looked more like a tryptophan molecule. She held a finger up and traced the shape in the air, then let her arm fall back down at her side.

Her legs felt jumpy, as if she could run for miles and not even be tired. She got out of bed and put her phone into her pajama-pants pocket. She yanked the window up, but before she could crawl out onto the fire escape, her bedroom door burst open and her siblings tumbled in.

"You can't go up to the REP without us!" Laney said, glaring at her. The REP, or Roof of Epic Proportions, was where the Vanderbeekers liked to hang out when they had important things to discuss.

"Yeah, not cool," Oliver chimed in.

"We're going with you," Hyacinth said in an uncharacteristically stubborn way, her hands on her hips.

Jessie glared back at her siblings. "How long have you been standing outside my door?"

"A super-long time," Laney said.

Jessie made a big production of being annoyed, but she was secretly glad for the company. Her bedroom was lonely with Isa gone. "Fine, let's go up."

"Oh goody!" Laney said, running across the room and climbing out the window first.

Laney was getting good at navigating the fire escape, but when she reached the second floor, she leaned down by Miss Josie and Mr. Jeet's window and peeked in. The curtains were still open from the day before, and the window was halfway raised.

"I can't believe it all happened only yesterday," Jessie said as she came up behind Laney. She took a deep breath, but she couldn't even get the slightest whiff of Miss Josie's Southern Rose perfume.

"Do you think Miss Josie's plants miss her?" Hyacinth asked.

"Plants don't have feelings," Jessie said. "They lack brains and nervous systems."

"Mr. Beiderman told me once that Luciana played the violin for her plants," Hyacinth said.

"I never knew Luciana did that," Oliver said.

"And Miss Josie always sings to them and touches the leaves," Hyacinth continued. "Why would they do that if plants don't have feelings?"

Jessie sniffed. "People believe tons of unscientific things."

Hyacinth stared into the apartment. "Maybe you should study that for the next science fair, because it sure does look like the plants miss her."

Jessie peered into the dark apartment, ready to discount Hyacinth's theory.

"Look at the seedlings!" Laney yelled, pointing at the trays. "They're dying!"

"They are not dying," Jessie said, but she took a closer look.

"They're dying," Oliver observed.

"I told you," Hyacinth said to Jessie. "They miss Miss Josie."

"They're just thirsty," Jessie said. "Come on, let's water them."

Oliver yanked up the window, and the kids jumped into the apartment.

"I don't like being here without them," Laney said.

Hyacinth looked around. "It's spooky. It doesn't smell right. And the plants miss their music."

"I can sing to them," Laney offered.

"NO," her siblings answered immediately.

Jessie snapped her fingers. "Let's get the music prodigy on the phone." She dug her cell out of her pocket and dialed, then put it on speaker.

Isa's panicked voice came out moments later. "Is Mr. Jeet okay? Oh my gosh, should I come home right now?"

"Isa, chill. He's fine."

A relieved sigh came through the phone. "Don't scare me like that. I thought it was an emergency. You never call me."

"Hi, Isa!" Laney said into the speaker. "Can you come back early? I miss you."

"I miss you too," Isa said.

Oliver leaned close to the phone. "I didn't even realize you were gone."

"Ha-ha, I miss you too, Oliver."

"We're in Miss Josie and Mr. Jeet's apartment," Jessie said. "Hyacinth thinks the plants are sad without them and need music. What about some violin?"

"It helps them grow," Hyacinth chimed in.

There was a pause; then Isa's voice buzzed through the phone. "Sure. Let me get my violin out."

Jessie grabbed the watering can from the kitchen counter and filled it up while Isa got her violin and listened to Laney, Hyacinth, and Oliver tell her all about the church garden project.

Jessie tried gently pouring water over the seedlings, but they had weak stems, and a lot of them collapsed. Hyacinth attempted to prop them up, but they flopped back down. A moment later, Isa began playing Borodin's "Nocturne" on her violin, and Hyacinth picked up the phone and brought it from seedling tray to seedling tray, and from plant to plant. Laney ran her hands over Miss Josie's larger plants like she had seen her neighbor do. The brownstone seemed to sigh with relief at the music, allowing a sweet summer breeze to come through the open window and flutter the curtains in a dance.

When Jessie said goodbye to Isa a few minutes later, another breeze drifted through the window.

She took a deep breath, and for a brief moment, she could feel Miss Josie's all-encompassing hug wrap around her.

THURSDAY, JUNE 28

Days Mr. Jeet in Hospital: 3

Days Until Garden
Extravaganza: 16

Eleven

The Vanderbeekers headed to the garden right after breakfast the next morning, armed with their new garden tools and some trash bags Oliver had taken from Papa's closet of superintendent supplies. They picked up Tilia of the Eternal Spring from where she had been hidden in a corner of the alley next to the brownstone, right behind the trash cans, and they arrived at the garden a little before nine o'clock. Yesterday, they had taken so much care to close the gate and rearrange the plants to cover up any hints of an opening that it took several minutes of rooting through the ivy to find the lock again.

Once inside, they surveyed the land.

"We can put the fountain over there," Laney said, pointing to the middle, around where the bathtub was.

"Who said we were getting a fountain?" Oliver asked.

"I thought it up right this minute," Laney said proudly.

Hyacinth showed Oliver where she wanted Tilia of the Eternal Spring to go—right next to the Silver Queen—and Oliver moved the tree off the hand truck and set it down in the designated spot.

"Let's get all the trash picked up before we do any planting," Jessie advised. She passed out the gardening gloves and trash bags and told the younger kids to watch out for broken glass and to be careful with what they touched. "And for goodness' sake, don't go anywhere near that toilet!" she added.

The kids got to work. Laney picked up a potato chip bag and Hyacinth picked up a plastic Coke bottle and threw it away. Oliver and Jessie grabbed trash and pulled weeds, and within half an hour, everyone was sweaty and the trash bag filled up.

They were weeding along the fence line that

bordered the sidewalk when they heard the staccato taps of shoes.

Oliver shushed his sisters. "It's Mr. Huxley!" he whispered.

The Vanderbeekers immediately froze.

The steps approached and stopped by the fence.

The kids took shallow breaths.

Then they heard clicking, the same sound Mama's and Papa's phones made when they used the camera.

There was rummaging in the ivy on the fence, as if Mr. Huxley was looking for something. Was he looking for the way in? Oliver hoped the opening had been concealed when he'd shut the gate. The ivy before the Vanderbeekers rustled while they inched away from where they thought Mr. Huxley was.

Finally, the movement on the other side of the fence stopped and they heard Mr. Huxley walk away. Which left the Vanderbeekers wondering: Why was Mr. Huxley so interested in the lot now? And was it just a happenstance that his interest coincided with their own?

✵ ✵ ✵

After a few minutes of waiting to see if Mr. Huxley would return, the Vanderbeekers got back to work. Oliver picked up another plastic bottle and threw it toward an open trash bag a few feet away. It missed by two inches. Oliver's spirits sank. He could already envision what position Coach would assign him on the basketball team: benchwarmer.

"Are we done yet?" Laney asked. She had settled herself on an empty milk crate under the silver maple tree, her hair plastered to her forehead. She scratched the insides of her arms, which always got super itchy in the summer humidity. The sun was burning hot, and Oliver wondered if they should go back home for sunscreen. This was a thought that had never once crossed his mind in his entire life, but one look at Laney made him think going home would be a good idea.

Jessie stood up from where she was pulling weeds and stretched her back. "This is going to take a while."

"I think it's getting cleaner," Hyacinth said, grabbing a weed and tugging it. The weed refused to budge. She yanked harder, putting all her weight into it, and the weed came loose and Hyacinth tumbled to the ground. "Is it lunchtime yet?" she asked, not making any move to get up.

Jessie looked at her watch. "It's eleven thirty. I think we can take a break."

"Yay!" Oliver said, then wiped his face with his sleeve.

The Vanderbeekers gathered up their tools, put them in an old paint bucket, and left it by Tilia. Oliver opened the gate slowly and peeked out.

"Coast clear," he reported. They filed out and pushed the gate closed again. Oliver, who had used the Internet the night before to research how to reset the lock, changed the combination to 0307, the month and day of Laney's birth, to make it more secure but still easy to remember.

They were a few steps away from the garden gate when Herman Huxley biked down the sidewalk. Oliver's mind raced. Had Herman seen them leave the garden?

Herman was wearing a pair of brand-new sneakers and riding his Eastern Racer 500. He braked when he got to them and let the wheels squeal. "What are you doing?"

"Nothing," Oliver said, unconsciously rubbing his scraped elbow.

"I saw you coming out of that gate. What's in there?"

Oliver's heart stuttered at the thought of being discovered. "None of your business."

Herman's face hardened. "Who wants to be in that toxic waste dump, anyways?"

"That's not a very nice thing to say," Hyacinth called from behind Jessie, where she was hiding.

"Whatever. I've got to get to robotics camp." Herman pushed off on his bike and raced down the street.

Oliver glared at him. Herman had no idea how good he had it: nice sneakers, awesome bike, and now robotics camp? It wasn't fair.

Oliver thought about their morning in the lot and had a moment of doubt. What if Herman was right about it being an irredeemable toxic waste pit?

❈ ❈ ❈

The kids returned home later that afternoon, and the second they opened the door, Franz pounced on

Hyacinth and licked her face as if they had been separated for years. Then Mama came out from the kitchen and took one glance at the state of her children. She clucked over their sunburns, the scratches on their arms and legs from the weeds, and the state of Laney's arms and neck, which were red and puckered from all the scratching she had done.

"What have you been doing all morning?" Mama cried.

"Picking up trash!" Laney said, scratching at her neck.

"We were helping clean the, uh, park," Jessie said, glancing at her siblings.

"It looks like you've been rolling around in thistles," Mama said. "Go take showers and I'll get lunch ready for you."

Oliver took the upstairs bathroom while the girls showered in the downstairs bathroom, and when they were clean, Mama tended to Laney's eczema flare-up with lotion to help with the itchiness. Finally, they sat down for lunch.

The kids sucked down huge glasses of water along with wraps Mama had made from tortillas filled with roast turkey, tomatoes, and lettuce. The food tasted so good! Jessie wanted to go upstairs and take a nap after her stomach was filled.

"Did you go to the hospital this morning?" Hyacinth asked.

"Uh-huh," Mama answered.

There was a long pause.

"How's Mr. Jeet?" Laney finally asked.

"When is he coming home?" Oliver said.

"I don't know," Mama said. "He's got a long recovery ahead of him."

"Two days?" Laney asked.

"Longer than that."

"A week?" Jessie asked.

"Maybe longer than that. I don't know," Mama said. "He can't rush it. Now tell me more about this park project."

Oliver raised his water glass to his mom. "That's a classic move."

Mama raised her eyebrows at him.

"What does that mean?" Laney said.

"It means," Jessie explained, "that Mama is really

good at changing the subject when there's an uncomfortable conversation."

A quiet fell over the table. Jessie swallowed the last bite of her sandwich. Mr. Jeet and Miss Josie had been gone for only two full days. Why did it feel so much longer?

Twelve

After lunch, Hyacinth ran upstairs to get her knitting supplies. Her yarn rope was getting out of control. She could tie it around the doorknob of her bedroom and trail it all the way down the stairs, through the living room, and to the basement! It was beautiful, her most impressive yarn project to date.

Hyacinth stuffed the project in her backpack, then reached for her knitting pouch and attached it to her belt. Inside the pouch were two sets of knitting needles in different sizes and two skeins of yarn, purple and green. This was the last of the yarn from Mama's collection, and Hyacinth wondered what she would do once it was all gone.

Hyacinth stepped outside her bedroom door and

went downstairs with Franz bumping his nose against her ankles. Her siblings were already waiting for her by the door. She clipped a leash to Franz's harness, and off they went.

When they got to the gate, Oliver opened the lock and the Vanderbeekers sneaked in. The garden welcomed them with a chorus of birdsong and a summer breeze that smelled like ripe strawberries and sunshine. Hyacinth put her backpack on the ground and picked up a spade from the paint bucket. She hummed as she worked, enjoying the way the cleared area was growing. Soon enough, bags filled with weeds were jumbled in a pile by the gate.

Jessie consulted her watch. "The garbage truck will be here in an hour. Hyacinth, can you put these trash bags by the curb?"

Hyacinth was ready for a knitting break anyway, so she put on her backpack and picked up the trash bags. Franz trailed after her, his leash dragging behind him. After opening the gate a tiny crack and seeing no one, she opened it wider and stepped onto the sidewalk with the bags. She threw them on the pile of garbage already in front of the church, then grabbed a plastic milk crate that had been put out for recycling. She walked back in front of the garden fence and sat on the upside-down milk crate. Franz lay next to her, rolling over so his belly was exposed to the sunshine, while Hyacinth took out her yarn and garland. She wove the end of the garland back around her fingers and got into a good knitting rhythm while the sun crept up the sky and warmed the neighborhood. She was about to switch yarn colors when a voice interrupted her peace.

"What are you working on?"

Hyacinth looked up and shaded her eyes against the sun.

It was Herman Huxley.

She looked back down at her knitting, hoping Herman would go away. His footsteps faded, but they returned only a minute later. A second milk crate was placed next to hers, and Herman sat down and leaned over to pet Franz.

"I thought you had robotics camp," Hyacinth said, squinting at him.

"It got canceled. Nice dog," he said, rubbing that special spot on Franz's belly that made his left leg twitch in happiness. "I used to knit with my hands like that, but now I like knitting with needles."

Hyacinth didn't say anything, but she unzipped her pouch and pulled out a set of knitting needles and some spring-green yarn and handed it to him.

"What are we making?" he asked.

Hyacinth shrugged, continuing her massive yarn garland.

Herman, in the meantime, was casting on stitches at a remarkable rate. Hyacinth was shocked. Here was a kid, just like her, who could knit!

Hyacinth wanted to say *Did you knock my brother down on purpose?* but instead she said, "I've been working on this rope for weeks. Maybe I'll enter it in the *Guinness Book of World Records* for longest yarn rope."

He didn't respond.

"Who taught you how to knit?" she asked.

"My mom."

"Do you think she can teach me to knit really fast like you?" Hyacinth asked.

"Probably not. She works for the United Nations,

so she's always working and traveling. She's never around."

"Oh."

"She taught me when I was five. My grandma said it was silly for her to teach a five-year-old boy how to knit, but I ended up liking it."

"My mom taught me too, but she's not that good. Sometimes I go upstairs and knit with Miss Josie."

Herman held up his knitting. He had transformed his green yarn into a four-leaf clover. He leaned over and tied the loose ends around her wrist to make a bracelet.

Before Hyacinth could say thank you, Herman said, "We should do some yarn bombing."

Hyacinth did not know what yarn bombing was. It sounded violent.

"It's like graffiti for knitters," Herman explained when he saw Hyacinth's uncertainty. "One time I knitted something to wrap around lampposts. Another time I covered some parking meters. The point is to make really industrial things look less depressing."

"Okay. How do we start?" Hyacinth asked.

"We can start easy, since it's your first time. How

about covering that post?" He pointed at the silver post holding up a sign that announced that street cleanings were on Tuesdays and Fridays from three to five in the afternoon.

Hyacinth looked at Herman. "That sounds good, but do we have enough yarn?"

"We don't have to cover the whole thing," he explained.

Hyacinth watched Herman cast on new stitches using the purple yarn. Then she thought, *Herman actually is pretty nice.*

⁂

Since they had a limited amount of yarn, Herman said goodbye after they attached the yarn bombing to the pole, and he went home. Hyacinth rejoined her siblings in the garden, where no one had even noticed she had been gone.

An hour later, much progress had been made, and they headed to the brownstone, where they found a note from Mama on the dining room table.

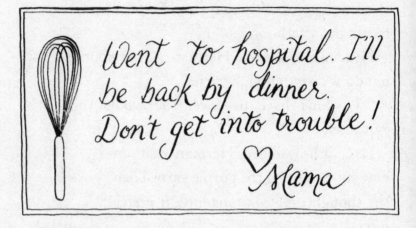

Went to hospital. I'll be back by dinner. Don't get into trouble!

♡ Mama

They had an hour before dinner, so Hyacinth and Laney decided to check in on Mr. Beiderman.

The two youngest Vanderbeekers went up the stairs. Franz trotted next to Hyacinth, his nails clicking against the wood staircase. When they got to the top floor, Hyacinth knocked on the door and Mr. Beiderman's voice rang out.

"Who is it?" a voice demanded.

"Hyacinth and Laney!" the girls chorused.

"Hold on! I'm . . . cleaning up."

A minute later, the door cracked open and Princess

Cutie squeezed out before it fully opened. Franz promptly licked the kitten's face, making the fur spike up on top of her head. Mr. Beiderman opened the door wider, and Laney sniffed the air suspiciously.

"I smell that meat-in-a-tin stuff," Laney reported, making a face.

"Oooh," Hyacinth said as she wagged a finger at Mr. Beiderman. "Mama is going to be mad at you!"

"You have no proof," Mr. Beiderman retorted. "That's just the smell of . . . turpentine. For my paintings."

"Uh-huh," Laney said, disbelieving. "I know that meat smell when I smell it."

Laney marched inside and made a beeline for the garbage can, where she found an empty SPAM tin under a magazine. She then inspected the lower cabinets until she came upon a secret stash of SPAM behind some canned beans. "You are good at hiding things," she told him. "Was Luciana good at it too?"

"She was . . . well, yes, she was very good at hiding things," Mr. Beiderman said.

Hyacinth and Laney stilled, hoping Mr. Beiderman would keep talking. Laney liked to ask about Luciana even though sometimes Mr. Beiderman did not want to talk about her.

"She loved burying things too," he continued, surprising the girls as he went on. "I used to take her to the playground when she was your age, and she would bury things in the sandbox and then forget she had done it. She was like a squirrel." Mr. Beiderman closed the cabinet doors and noticed that Laney's neck was covered with scratches. "What happened to your neck? And did you get sunburned?"

Laney squinted at him. "Are you changing the subject?"

Mr. Beiderman glared at her.

"We were outside all day," Laney said hurriedly.

"Doing what?" Mr. Beiderman asked.

"Oh, you know," Hyacinth said.

Mr. Beiderman narrowed his eyes, but Hyacinth refused to reveal anything.

"I was wondering," Laney began as she stacked the SPAM tins in a pyramid on the table, "do you think plants and flowers like music? Jessie says no because they're not nervous."

"They don't have nervous *systems*," Hyacinth corrected her.

"Isa played violin music for Miss Josie's plants yesterday, and they loved it," Laney said.

"Luciana had a window box full of lavender in her bedroom," said Mr. Beiderman. "She used to play the violin for them all the time. She said it made plants grow better."

"You want to come with us tomorrow to Ms. Hiba's store and buy some lavender?" Laney asked.

"I . . . can't," Mr. Beiderman said.

Hyacinth could tell Laney was getting ready for a big counterargument, so she said, "It's okay, Mr. Beiderman. Mama always says healing takes time."

And she curled up on the couch next to him and they looked ahead at the wall, which was covered with black-and-white paintings Mr. Beiderman had made of his wife and daughter over the course of many years after their deaths. Princess Cutie hopped lightly onto his lap and curled up against his stomach, purring. Hyacinth leaned her head on his shoulder, and Laney cuddled up on his other side.

Death had never been real to Hyacinth, but now, with Mr. Jeet being so sick, she could understand a tiny bit of Mr. Beiderman's loss. She felt Mr. Beiderman's shaky breaths, and she wondered how his heart could keep beating and how his lungs could keep drawing in air even though he'd lost the two people he loved most in the world.

Thirteen

That night, as Oliver chewed the quinoa and spinach salad at dinner, he thought about what life had been like just three days earlier, back when Mama had made real desserts, like butterscotch cookies and gooey chocolate brownies. When he could hear Mr. Jeet and Miss Josie puttering around upstairs, the sound from their evening game shows drifting through the brownstone and their laughter bringing life to the building.

Now the brownstone was so hauntingly quiet that Oliver felt suffocated. He needed to get out. His breath came out in a whoosh as he pushed his chair back abruptly. "Can I go visit Angie?" Mama glanced at him, surprised, but after one concerned quirk of an eyebrow, she let him go.

Oliver raced out of the brownstone and skidded to a stop on the sidewalk. He gulped in the cooler air. Instead of going to Angie's place, he went to the back of the brownstone, squeezed by the trash cans, and entered the backyard through the side gate. He climbed the ladder to his treehouse. If Jimmy L were around, they could talk on their walkie-talkies. He looked across the yard at the brownstone where his friend lived; the bedroom would be empty for the next three weeks. Oliver was careful not to look toward his own brownstone—he knew the second floor would be dark and empty.

Oliver lay down on the wooden platform, running his hands over the smooth planks Uncle Arthur had carefully sanded so Oliver wouldn't get any splinters, and stared at the branches above him. The leaves rustled in the wind, and the sounds of Harlem filled his ears. People down the street were grilling in their backyard, their chatter a low rumble. A dog two doors down barked from a terrace, and the sirens of a passing ambulance pierced the night.

It could have been five minutes or maybe an hour, but the next thing he knew, it was much darker, and someone—probably one of his sisters—was climbing up the rope. Oliver rolled over onto his stomach and looked down over the platform.

"Leave me alone!" he yelled.

"Geez, Oliver, what a welcome." The voice of his friend Angie rang through the darkness.

Oliver let out a breath. A second later, Angie's head popped over the side of the platform.

"What's up?" she asked as she settled next to him. She pulled a bulging bag off her back and put it between them. "I heard about Mr. Jeet. I figured you could use some company." Angie unzipped the bag and pulled out two cans of grape soda, three packs of sour straws, and some cookies. "The cookies aren't like your mom's," she apologized.

Oliver popped open a can of soda and took a deep drink. "Oh yeah, that is so good." He paused, enjoying the artificial flavors filling his mouth. "Mama wants us all to eat really healthy now. The Mr. Jeet thing really freaked her out, so she is on a total health kick. I had *quinoa* for dinner." Oliver shuddered.

"When can he come home?" Angie asked, peeling open the sour straws and offering one to Oliver.

Oliver took a straw and bit into it. "Mama doesn't know. She keeps bringing clothes to Miss Josie because she won't leave his side."

"It's so romantic," Angie said. "They are totally that couple who always hold hands even though they've been together for fifty years."

Oliver shrugged. "I guess." He bit into a sour straw. "Wow, this all tastes *so* good."

"We can put the rest in your bin," Angie said, pointing to the wooden bin that held snacks, flashlights, his walkie-talkie, and other outdoor-survival essentials.

A long silence followed. Oliver wondered if he should tell Angie about the garden. It was supposed to be secret, but this was *Angie.*

"Can I tell you something?" Oliver finally said.

When Angie nodded, Oliver told her about how he and his sisters had discovered a way into the abandoned lot next to the church, and their big plans for transforming it. He related how they'd pooled their money and bought gardening tools, and how he wasn't sure how they would afford to buy plants to create Mr. Jeet and Miss Josie's dream garden.

"Come on, we can think of a way to raise money,"

Angie said. She put an index finger to each temple. "I've got it. Let's have a bake sale."

"Mama banned sugar. She thinks it will make us sick."

"Car wash."

"No one would *ever* trust us to wash their cars."

"Hyacinth can make dog treats to sell."

"No one would— Hey, actually, that's a good idea."

"We can sell other things too . . . Hold on! A brilliant idea popped into my brain," said Angie. "We can have a sidewalk sale! I have a ton of picture books I don't read anymore."

Oliver thought about the things in his tiny bedroom. Could he bear to sell some of his books?

"I'll come by tomorrow morning after math," Angie said. "We only have an hour of class on Fridays, so I'll be back at ten fifteen. Our building has some folding tables we can set everything up on. Now tell me what else is bothering you."

Oliver narrowed his eyes. "Nothing."

Angie gave him a do-you-think-I-was-born-yesterday look. "C'mon, I know when something is up. Tell me."

"You're not going to be able to help or solve it or anything."

"Who cares? I just want to know."

There were so many things bothering him. So he told Angie about how they had snuck into the hospital and how Mr. Jeet looked like he was dying and how there were three tick marks under "Bad Days" on his health chart. He shared how Herman Huxley had called the garden a toxic waste pit, and how he couldn't get that image out of his mind.

What Oliver did not share was why it was so important for him to finish the garden.

Angie was a good listener and didn't interrupt him. When he was done talking, they lay down and stared up at the sky through the leaves. They couldn't see many stars in New York City—too much light pollution—but Oliver liked the way the leaves were silhouetted against the dark sky. They rustled in the wind, and Oliver imagined that his wishes for the garden were being blown across Harlem, spreading out among the brownstones and buildings and resting upon the millions of other stories and wishes that made up the neighborhood.

❋ ❋ ❋

It was no surprise to Jessie that she had trouble sleeping again. It was so quiet in the brownstone. No Isa lying in the bed across from her, whispering to her about the day. No footsteps above her from the second floor as Miss Josie and Mr. Jeet shuffled around, getting ready for bed.

Jessie pulled up the window and stepped out onto the fire escape. She started up the stairs, toward the roof. She had just reached Miss Josie and Mr. Jeet's darkened apartment when the window abruptly raised and a voice yelled, "Stop, thief!"

Jessie's foot slipped and she grabbed the railing, but the leaves sticking to the metal slats made the fire escape especially slippery. "Fudge!" she shrieked as she lost traction and skidded down a few steps. She imagined tumbling down the rickety stairs and crashing to the ground.

"Geez, help me out a little?" the voice from the second-floor apartment said.

Only then did Jessie realize that the hand attached to the voice was wrapped around her arm and was pulling her back. She tumbled through the window and landed in a heap on the floor in Miss Josie's kitchen.

A hulking figure loomed above her.

Jessie blinked and looked up, but the apartment was shadowy and dark.

Then the hulking figure spoke, with a slight Southern accent. "Jessie?"

Fourteen

Jessie's eyes adjusted to the darkness in Miss Josie and Mr. Jeet's apartment as she peered at the person who had just saved her from tumbling down the fire escape. How did he know her name? That voice was so familiar . . .

"Jessie, it's me. Orlando."

Jessie scrambled up. "Orlando? What are *you* doing here?"

Orlando was Mr. Jeet's grandnephew. Three years ago, Orlando had spent the summer living with the Jeets. He loved science and was the same age as Jessie, and they were glued at the hip for three months. Orlando had brought with him a whole pack of litmus paper, and they roamed the neighborhood, testing mango juice from the man selling peeled mangos from his cart, puddle water after a rain, and the remains of melted shaved ice on a hot day. They'd learned a lot about acids and bases that summer.

Orlando flicked on the light, and Jessie got a good look at him. "Holy smokes, you look like a football player!" The last time she'd seen him, he was short and skinny and carried a magnifying glass in his shirt pocket.

Orlando laughed. "I'm hungry all the time. And I play football," he admitted.

Jessie staggered back and clutched her heart. "Tell me it's not true."

"What? It's a big thing in Georgia."

"I guess you can be a football player *and* a scientist. Are you staying with Miss Josie and Mr. Jeet again? Didn't you hear they're in the hospital?" Jessie said.

"I know. And I'm here for good. Ma got a nursing job at Montefiore Hospital, so we packed up our apartment in Georgia and moved down the street. I stopped by because I still have a key to their place, and Ma wanted me to drop off groceries for them. I was going to wait until tomorrow to come say hi to y'all."

"That is the best news! What school are you going to in the fall?"

Orlando grinned. "I guess whatever school you're going to."

"We can be science lab partners! Ooh, I need to show you something, but let me water Miss Josie's plants first."

"I already did," Orlando said.

Jessie leaned over to look at the seedlings. "Hey, these look so much better! Yesterday when we came by, they were all droopy."

"I trimmed some of the weaker ones. Aunt Josie always puts a few seeds in each compartment, just in case, but there's only room for one strong plant in each cell."

Jessie looked at Orlando. "You know about plants?"

Orlando shrugged. "In Georgia I worked at the farm down the street during the summers."

Jessie studied him. If he helped them, that would mean opening up the garden beyond the four Vanderbeekers.

Orlando caught Jessie staring, so he crossed his eyes and blew out his cheeks like a bullfrog.

Jessie laughed.

"You know," he said, "you haven't changed a bit. Your brain is always going at warp speed."

Jessie took that as a compliment. She headed back to the window. "C'mon, follow me." She popped outside and onto the fire escape. When Orlando didn't follow, she leaned down to look through the window. "You coming?"

Orlando was skeptical. "Will this thing hold me?"

Jessie jumped up and down on it. It only rattled a little bit. "Sure. Sometimes all my siblings are on it at the same time."

"I'm not too fond of heights," he told her, not moving from the apartment. "I don't know why you New Yorkers want to live miles off the ground."

"Fine. Don't come if you're scared," Jessie said, heading up.

She wasn't surprised to hear Orlando climb out the window behind her. She looked back at him, and he was gripping the skinny rail as if his life depended on it. The steps were narrow, so he could get only part of his sneaker on each step.

They went up past Mr. Beiderman's apartment, then climbed onto the roof.

"Whoa . . ." Orlando said when he reached the top and got his first look out over Harlem. He followed Jessie around the perimeter of the roof, seeing the city from all angles. When he got to the area where a funnel was attached to a strange metal structure, he checked over the side of the roof to see where it led.

"Oh, hey," he said. "Rube Goldberg machine, right? I built an *epic* one for our science fair. It fed our cat every morning at six."

"I'd like to see that," Jessie said.

"I have a video, but we had to leave the machine back home. Show me how this thing works."

Jessie had a supply of filled two-liter bottles of water by the edge of the roof, so she uncapped one and set it upside down so the water flowed into the funnel and engaged a series of wind chimes and a rain stick. Music swirled around them.

"Nice!" Orlando said.

"I made it for Isa. She's at music camp for three

weeks. It's hard for her to be away from Mr. Jeet and Miss Josie right now, though."

"I heard you were there when he had the stroke. Was it awful?"

Jessie looked out over Harlem. The lights twinkled back at her. "I thought he was dying." Thinking about Mr. Jeet made her feel like an elephant was stepping on her chest, so she changed the subject. "Do you miss Georgia?"

Orlando looked up at the sky. "I miss the bigness of the sky. Here it seems as small as a postage stamp. I really miss the stars. I loved feeling as if the stars could fall down right on top of me. Here it's like stars don't even exist."

Orlando's phone beeped, and he pulled it out of his jeans pocket and sighed. "My ma. Let me text her." Orlando spoke out loud as he texted her back. "I'm fine. Coming home." Then he said to Jessie, "Gotta go."

"See you tomorrow?" Jessie said.

"I promised Ma I'd help her unpack in the morning, but I'll come by after. Give me your phone." After they plugged their numbers into each other's phones, they walked to the fire escape and descended. When Orlando got to Miss Josie and Mr. Jeet's apartment, he climbed in through the window. Jessie passed by him and started to go down the steps to her bedroom.

"Jessie?" he called out.

"Yeah?" she said.

"It's good to see you again."

Jessie smiled and turned back to say the same. But Orlando had already pulled down Miss Josie and Mr. Jeet's window, and the only response from the night was the sound of a distant car alarm, ringing out in rhythmic bursts that matched her heartbeat exactly.

Friday, June 29

Days Mr. Jeet in Hospital: 4

Days Until the Garden
Extravaganza: 15

Fifteen

Oliver spent the morning going through his stuff, looking for things he could contribute to the yard sale. It pained him to give away any of his books, but he did manage to find seven he could *maybe* part with. Other items for the yard sale: an old catcher's mitt, a set of superhero action figures, and some collared shirts and pants (that still had the tags on them) that he found hanging in his closet.

He had gone around to his sisters that morning to explain the sidewalk-sale plan, and they'd agreed it was the best way to raise funds for the garden. Laney and Jessie worked on a sign, and Hyacinth packed up little bags of the dog and cat treats she had baked.

Mama was back at the hospital, helping Miss Josie

fill out insurance paperwork, and Papa was at work. No one had heard from Mr. Beiderman; sometimes he spent the day painting in his apartment and refused to open the door no matter how long the Vanderbeekers knocked.

At ten fifteen sharp, the doorbell rang, and Oliver opened it to find Angie standing outside.

"Ready?" she asked. "My neighbor helped me carry a folding table to the sidewalk already."

Oliver called to his sisters, who crashed down the stairs with bags of stuff and a huge sign. Franz followed, holding a dirty tennis ball in his mouth.

"Look what I got!" Laney opened a bag for Angie and Oliver to see. Inside were a bulging pouch of rocks and seashells, six headbands with enormous bows on them, and a few mostly empty notebooks. "Those headbands squish my head," she told them. "I'm going to get a hundred dollars for them so I can buy roses for the garden."

Oliver raised his eyebrows, but Angie shoved her elbow into his side before he could respond.

"We definitely need plants, but I think our first priority should be good soil," Jessie said. "Miss Josie always talks about how important soil is."

The Vanderbeekers lugged their stuff to the sidewalk and promptly got into a fight about how everything was going to be displayed. Laney wanted her stuff in the prime real estate at the front of the table, but Jessie argued that Oliver's books would sell better and should be placed more prominently. Oliver didn't want his books to be seen—he was having doubts about selling them—so he discreetly rearranged the merchandise while Jessie was occupied trying to locate potential customers.

Oliver didn't need to worry about his books, because

their block was strangely deserted. Sure, it was ten thirty on a Friday morning, but was it always this quiet? The Vanderbeekers and Angie stood behind their table; the only sound was Franz gnawing on his tennis ball.

"I'm sure people will come by soon," Hyacinth asserted, and she was right. Mr. Jones was making his way down the street with his USPS mail cart, and he waved to the Vanderbeekers as he approached.

"'Awesome Stuff for Sale,'" he read from the sign. Then he took his time looking through the offerings. "What are you raising money for?"

"Flowers," Laney said immediately.

"Um," Jessie said, glancing at her siblings, "it's for neighborhood beautification."

"Ah," Mr. Jones said. "Flowers around the street trees would be nice."

"Uh-huh," the Vanderbeekers and Angie replied.

Mr. Jones took a few more minutes perusing the table. "I'm afraid there's not much here I can use," he said after picking up and putting down a headband.

"That's my favorite," Laney said.

"I'd be up for some more dog treats, though," Mr.

Jones said, glancing at the basket of pet treats. He pulled his wallet out.

"It's two bucks a bag," Oliver said, but Hyacinth shushed him.

"No way are you paying for dog treats," she said. "You have complimentary status for life."

"But—" Oliver and Mr. Jones protested.

"Nope," Hyacinth interrupted firmly, waving a hand in front of her. "How many bags do you want?"

"Oh, just one," Mr. Jones said.

"Here's five," Hyacinth said. "You should try these cat treats too. Want some for Pinky Pye?" Pinky Pye was Mr. Jones's eighteen-year-old tabby cat. Hyacinth shoved three bags of cat treats into Mr. Jones's mail bag.

"Worst salesperson ever," Oliver mumbled, and Angie and Jessie shrugged in a that's-Hyacinth gesture.

"Thank you much," he said. "Pinky Pye will right enjoy these."

When Mr. Jones had rolled his cart out of earshot, Oliver hissed, "Pinky Pye doesn't even have teeth! How is she going to eat those?"

Hyacinth pursed her lips. "I don't want to take his money, okay? He works really hard."

"Fine," Oliver said. Then he watched as five more people bought nothing but received complimentary dog and cat treats. "Our business model is a disaster."

Angie, who was a girl of action, came up with a new plan. "Maybe we need to hand-sell our stuff," she suggested. "We can bring some things with us and knock on doors in my building. There are seventy-seven units, and lots of people are retired and should be home now."

Oliver consulted with his sisters, and everyone agreed there was no harm in trying. He grabbed one of the boxes and put in some books, his fancy clothes, three headbands, two unidentifiable knitting projects Hyacinth had made, a couple of outdated space books (one still acknowledged poor Pluto as a planet), and five glass animal figurines Jessie had found at the bottom of her desk drawer.

"We'll be back!" Angie called; then she and Oliver walked two buildings down. Angie let them into the building with her key. "Let's start at the top and work our way to the bottom."

Oliver was huffing by the time they made it up to the fifth floor in the walk-up building. Angie knocked on Apartment 5A, but there was no answer. In 5B, old Mr. Sayed bought Oliver's copy of *Gulliver's Travels* for a dollar after picking up and scrutinizing every item in the box for ten minutes. No answers in 5C or 5D, but in 5E Miss Monique bought three headbands for her three-year-old daughter, Natasha, who promptly put them all on at the same time. In 5F, Mrs. Guerrero bought Oliver's fancy clothes for her eight-year-old grandson, Emilio.

Angie and Oliver were feeling proud of their sales, but just as they raised their hands to knock on 5G, the door to 5H across the hallway banged open. A woman with blindingly white hair sticking out in all directions filled the doorway. She shook her walking stick at them in fury.

"Hooligans!" she shouted at the top of her lungs.

"Get behind me," Angie ordered Oliver.

Oliver obeyed instantly. "Should we make a run for it?" he whispered.

Angie turned her head slightly and said, "I've got this." She turned back to the lady and raised her hands in innocence. "Mrs. Archer, it's me, Angie. The super's daughter."

"Hooligans!" she shouted again, waving her stick. "I'm callin' the police, that's what I'm gonna do."

"Mrs. Archer, it's okay. We're just selling some things to raise money for a garden—"

"I'M CALLIN' THE POLICE!" Mrs. Archer screeched, grabbing her cell phone from the pocket of her housedress.

"You're right, let's run!" Angie said to Oliver, bolting for the stairs before he could even register what was happening.

Oliver, who was burdened with the box of sale items, couldn't move as fast and got a smack on his calf from Mrs. Archer's walking stick before he escaped.

Around floor three, Angie got the giggles, and Oliver started laughing too. When they finally burst out the back doors to the courtyard, they collapsed on the ground, laughing hysterically.

"Oh no," Angie said between gasps. "Did she get you with her walking stick?"

"Yes, she did, and thanks for abandoning me!"

Oliver said, rubbing his calf. "Man, she's brutal! I'll probably get a bruise."

"She's super protective of the building. She's lived here for over fifty years."

Oliver shook his head. "No kidding! Also—just a suggestion—I don't think we should go door-to-door anymore."

"Okay." Angie got up and held a hand out to Oliver. She pulled him to his feet, then froze.

"What's up?" Oliver asked.

"You need soil, right?"

"Right."

Angie pointed to a corner of the courtyard. Stacked along the side on pallets were bags and bags of garden soil.

Sixteen

The sidewalk sale was not going well, but Jessie forgot all about the money they weren't making the second she saw what was piled on a hand truck that Angie and Oliver were pulling behind them.

"We have soil!" Angie announced. "You're very welcome."

"Where did you get that?" Jessie asked, suspicious.

"In the courtyard of our building," Angie said. "And there are eighty more bags back there."

Jessie's eyes narrowed. "Are we allowed to use it?"

Angie beamed a brilliant smile. "Why not? It's been sitting outside for six months. The building manager wanted to put in a garden border around the courtyard, but then the company that was going to break up the concrete went bankrupt and the building owner couldn't find a more affordable quote. Better not to let the soil go to waste, right?"

Jessie bit her lip. "Don't you think we should ask your dad if we can use it?"

"Oh, he won't even notice," Angie answered. "Plus, he's in a special training today for trash-compactor maintenance, and he said only to call with emergencies with a capital *E*. My neighbor Señora Alvas is my responsible adult while he's gone, but she takes a nap from ten to twelve every day."

Jessie relented. "All right, if you're *sure* he'll be okay with it. Now, how are we going to get all this soil down the street to the garden?"

"Hey, y'all!" a voice called out. Jessie whipped around, and there was Orlando.

"Orlando!" Oliver, Angie, and Hyacinth yelled. Laney was too young to have known Orlando, but since everyone else was excited about him, she was too.

"What's up with all the soil?" he asked.

The Vanderbeekers and Angie looked at one another and held a silent conversation. A few eyebrow raises later, a decision was made.

"Can you keep a secret?" Jessie asked.

※ ※ ※

Oliver and Angie were put in charge of transporting soil using the hand truck. Hyacinth brought out their red Radio Flyer wagon, and Orlando loaded it up with bags. Laney wanted to ride on the wagon on top of the soil, but no one thought *that* was a good idea. It was agreed that Jessie would pull the wagon and Hyacinth and Laney would push. As a concession, Jessie said that after they dropped the first load of soil off at the garden, Laney could ride the empty wagon back down the street to pick up more. Orlando carried two soil bags at a time, one under each arm, which amazed everyone.

Thankfully, no one really paid much attention to a bunch of kids lugging bags of soil down 141st Street. This was New York City, and people were used to stranger things happening.

On the last transport of soil, right when Oliver, Angie, and Jessie were developing blisters from pulling the hand truck and the wagon, Benjamin came around the corner of 141st Street, whistling and carrying a huge bag with "Castleman's Bakery" stamped on it.

"Please tell me you have cheese croissants, and that they're for us!" Oliver yelled. His hands were killing him.

"I have cheese croissants, and they're for you guys!" Benjamin called back.

"I love you, Benny!" Laney said.

A small mountain of soil now sat piled up by the fence.

"What's this?" Benjamin asked.

The Vanderbeekers exchanged glances.

"Can you keep a secret?" Oliver asked.

"Of course," Benjamin said.

"Help us get this soil inside first, so we don't attract any more attention."

"Inside where?" Benjamin began, but then Oliver clicked open the lock and pushed in the gate.

"Whoa," Benjamin, Angie, and Orlando said in unison.

"It's like a fairy garden," Angie said. "Or an enchanted forest."

"What's with the bathtub and the toilet?" Benjamin asked.

"These weeds are epic," Orlando noted.

They dragged the soil through the gate and piled it up along the inside of the fence. It turned out the bags made excellent seats, and they all settled down and ripped open the bakery bag. The smell of croissants and cinnamon rolls and turnovers spilled out, and everyone made a grab for their favorite pastry.

For five minutes, there was only the sound of *mmm*s and *yum*s. Then, just as everyone had expected, Benjamin asked about Isa.

"She's fine, and no, she hasn't met another guy at orchestra camp," Jessie replied around a mouthful of cheese croissant.

Benjamin flushed, grabbed another apple turnover, and changed the subject. "So what's the plan with this place?"

"We're going to make it into a garden paradise," Laney said.

"We've already cleaned out two huge bags of trash," Oliver added.

"It's going to be awesome," Jessie said.

Laney stood up on the soil mountain and stretched her fingers to the sky. "It's going to be the garden of Mr. Jeet and Miss Josie's dreams!"

Seventeen

After they polished off all the pastries, Benjamin went back to work at the bakery for the afternoon, Angie went home to check in with Señora Alvas and to work on her math homework, and Orlando ran some errands for his mom. They each promised to return the next day, Saturday, to help distribute the soil. The Vanderbeekers headed home to eat a real lunch and to see if Mama had any Mr. Jeet news.

When they arrived, they were surprised to find Papa lying on the couch, groaning.

"I pulled my back carrying ten years' worth of Mr. Beiderman's old electronics out of his apartment," Papa explained.

"Does it hurt a lot?" Hyacinth asked, leaning down and kissing his cheek.

"Yes," he replied.

"Don't baby him!" Mama called from the kitchen. "He's fine!"

"I need to go to the emergency room," Papa called, but he winked at Hyacinth while he said it.

Mama had lunch spread out for them, and the kids descended on the food while Franz snuffled the floor for scraps and George Washington hopped on the table and tried to swipe a slice of cheese.

"How's Mr. Jeet?" Oliver asked before biting into his super-duper deli sandwich.

"He's fine! Just fine!" she said in her fake-happy voice.

The Vanderbeeker kids exchanged looks. Oliver sighed and went to the chalkboard.

✵ ✵ ✵

After lunch, they got ready to leave again.

"Where are you disappearing to all day?" Mama

asked as she pulled a load of laundry from the dryer. She had been washing Miss Josie's laundry for her and bringing fresh clothes to the hospital every day.

"The park, the playground . . . you know," Jessie said vaguely.

Mama eyed Papa. "You should go with them and get some fresh air. It's a beautiful day."

The Vanderbeeker kids froze. If Papa came with them, they would actually have to go to the playground instead of their garden.

"I'm injured!" Papa reminded her. He didn't budge from his spot on the couch.

"He needs rest and ibuprofen," Hyacinth suggested. She ran to the bathroom to get the medicine and was back in five seconds.

"Thank you, sweetie," Papa said. "I'm glad someone understands my pain."

Hyacinth leashed Franz, his tail at 150 wags per minute, or wpm, and then she and her siblings went out the door. Orlando was already on the stoop having a conversation with Mr. Beiderman, who was hanging out one of the third-floor windows.

"Where are you going?" Mr. Beiderman was yelling down to Orlando.

"Just for a walk, sir!" Orlando yelled up at him.

"Hi, Mr. Beiderman!" Hyacinth yelled.

"I don't want to see any more skinned knees, you hear?" Mr. Beiderman said. "And take these gloves with you, just in case!" Before anyone could register what was happening, gardening gloves—really nice ones with rubber grips and elastic around the wrist—rained down around them. Mr. Beiderman had thrown them from the third floor.

"Wow! Thanks, Mr. B!" the kids chorused, casting puzzled looks at one another. Was this just coincidence? Hyacinth wanted to ask how Mr. Beiderman knew they were gardening, but he had already disappeared from sight and she heard the window slam. She shrugged at her siblings, and they went down the street toward the church.

"When do you want the garden to be ready?" Orlando asked.

Jessie shrugged. "In time for Isa to get home in two weeks. But now I'm not sure Mr. Jeet will be back by then."

"He'll be back," Oliver said with certainty. "He has to be."

"I think we can get the main part done," Orlando said. "It'll be a lot of work, though."

"I can't wait to plant Tilia of the Eternal Spring," Hyacinth said.

"And Paganini food," Laney chimed in, bouncing from foot to foot.

"We've got to get rid of all the weeds first," Jessie said. "Then we can talk about what we should plant."

Oliver let them inside the gate and they got to work. Hyacinth noticed that it was a lot easier to pull weeds and pick up trash with the nice gardening gloves on. How had Mr. Beiderman known they needed them?

Hyacinth was working near the fence line with Laney, ripping out a particularly stubborn weed, when she heard the telltale clicks of fancy shoes.

She froze.

"What's wrong?" Laney asked as she sifted through the dirt to look for pretty rocks for her collection.

Hyacinth put her finger to her lips. Laney shrugged and continued her search. Hyacinth looked around for her siblings, but they were working on the far side of the lot and she didn't want to shout for them. The fancy-shoe taps were joined by more footsteps, which sounded like thuds.

Mr. Huxley's voice drifted through the fence. He sounded like the high string of Isa's violin when it was tightened too much. "As you can see, this area would be perfect for a multiple-family housing development."

Hyacinth took a breath, channeled Hyacinth the Brave, and moved her ear closer to the fence line.

"It's definitely a good-sized lot for a condominium complex." This voice was low and gruff. "I looked up the zoning. It all checks out. I already spoke to our lawyers, and they want to settle the closing on July sixteenth. That work for you?"

Hyacinth puffed out her cheeks. That was two days after the Garden Extravaganza!

Another voice—this man sounded like the rich banker in *Mary Poppins*—spoke. "Condos are hot property right now. We could do it up, make it really luxury, then sell it for four, five million. If we get an early buyer, we can even design it to their specifications, which means more cash."

Mr. Huxley cleared his throat. "Let's go to my office and discuss the details."

The three men's voices and footsteps faded away, and Hyacinth didn't dare move until she couldn't hear their voices anymore.

Laney was holding a rock two inches from her face, staring at it intently. Then she asked, "Why do they want to sell our garden?"

✦ ✦ ✦

Hyacinth was too upset to talk, but Laney was more than willing to share what they had just overheard.

"There were three guys, and one of them was Mr. Huxley. I could tell because he has that really squeaky voice. The other two guys I didn't get to see because they were on the other side of the fence." Laney made her voice go down as far as it would go. "But *they* had deep voices like this."

"Can you get to the point?" Oliver interjected.

"And all three of them said they could build a house

on top of our garden and it would sell for forty-five billion dollars!"

"Holy smokes," Jessie said at the same time that Orlando whistled.

"Four or five million, not forty-five billion," Hyacinth said through her tears. "They want to sell it on July sixteenth.

"Triple J wouldn't have let us have this land if they were selling it," Jessie said. "He said we could use it."

"Mr. Huxley said it," Hyacinth wailed. "What will happen to Miss Josie and Mr. Jeet's garden?"

Oliver picked up a rock and threw it at the vine-covered fence across the lot. "There's only one way to find out. We've got to ask Triple J."

Jessie pulled out her phone and dialed Triple J. "It's ringing," she told everyone, then, "It's going to voice mail." There was a pause, and Jessie said into the phone, "Hi, Triple J. I'm sorry to bother you, but we just overheard Mr. Huxley say he was going to sell the land next to the church. Is that true? Because you said we could use it to make a community garden, and we've already started on it . . . Anyways, can you call us back?"

Jessie clicked the phone off and looked at Orlando and her siblings.

Now what?

*   *   *

That night after dinner, the Vanderbeekers sat upstairs in Jessie and Isa's room. Triple J had not called them back.

"I know which building Herman lives in," Oliver said. "He's right by the school. We could visit Mr. Huxley and interrogate him." He imagined pulling Mr. Huxley into a dimly lit room and sitting him down on a solitary chair with a naked lightbulb hanging overhead while the Vanderbeekers conducted a cross-examination.

"Triple J wouldn't let him sell the land without telling us," Hyacinth said. "Or would he?"

"He *just* told us the garden was a good idea," Jessie said. "Why would he say that if it was going to be destroyed?"

"That's true," Oliver said. "There's no way they're selling it."

The Vanderbeekers looked around at one another, uncertain.

"Isa will know what to do," Jessie finally decided. She took out her phone and dialed, putting it on speaker. When Isa answered, Jessie explained everything.

"Sounds like it's just speculation," Isa said after she had heard the whole story. "How could Mr. Huxley sell the land without Triple J around? That doesn't make sense. Personally, I think the faster you can get the garden beautiful, the better. Not only will it be ready for Mr. Jeet and Miss Josie, but only a heartless grub would put a building on top of a community garden."

"Thanks, Isa," Jessie said.

Isa's voice filled the speakerphone. "I've got to go. There's a bonfire tonight, and I want to get there before the marshmallows and chocolate are all gone!"

Jessie hung up and looked out at her siblings. "We need to make this garden so gorgeous that Mr. Jeet and Miss Josie will love it and no one will tear it down. We have two weeks. Ideas, anyone?"

SATURDAY, JUNE 30

Days Mr. Jeet in Hospital: 5

Days Until Garden
Extravaganza: 14

Eighteen

The next morning, the Vanderbeekers trooped back over to the garden. It was a peaceful Saturday morning on 141st Street. Oliver liked it when the neighborhood was quiet, as though they were the only ones awake in Harlem. They took their time going down the street, stopping to point at flowers that might look good in the garden and waving at dogs that sat with their noses pressed to the windows, their tails wagging.

Oliver felt buoyed by the new sense of purpose. They were going to make the best garden in Harlem, and everyone was going to love it! He was so wrapped up in the dream of garden grandeur that he forgot to look before reaching for the lock.

"Hey!"

The Vanderbeekers spun around to see Herman Huxley running across the street, his bike next to him. Franz pulled on the leash to say hi.

"What are *you* doing here?" Oliver said.

"I wanted to give this to Hyacinth," Herman said, patting Franz on the head. He held up a bag.

"Thanks, Herman!" Hyacinth said, reaching for the bag.

Oliver blocked Hyacinth from grabbing it. "You don't know what's in there."

"It's yarn," Herman told them.

"Thank you so much!" Hyacinth said from behind Oliver.

"Wait. How do you know Hyacinth loves yarn?" Oliver asked, suspicious.

Hyacinth stepped past Oliver and took the bag. She opened it, and inside were the most beautiful, most vibrant yarns she had ever seen. They were like those exotic colors she found in the box of 120 Crayola crayons Mama and Papa had given her for her birthday: Sunset Orange, Atomic Tangerine, Sunglow, Mountain Meadow, Cornflower, Wild Blue Yonder, Purple

Mountains' Majesty, Razzle Dazzle Rose, and Mauvelous.

"We knit together," Hyacinth told Oliver. "Well, we knit together on Thursday. He's *really* good. Oh, Herman, thank you for this! There are so many colors! Are you sure you don't need them?"

"Wait," Oliver said again. "You guys are *friends?*"

Jessie's and Laney's heads whipped back and forth as the two tried to keep up with the conversation.

Hyacinth looked at Herman. Herman looked at Hyacinth.

"Yup," Hyacinth said.

Herman looked back at Oliver, a smile creeping onto his face. "Yup."

"Well, it was good seeing you," Oliver said to Herman. He looked at his wrist as if he were checking the time, but he wasn't wearing his watch. "We've got to go."

"But what about—" Hyacinth began.

"I thought we were going to—" Laney started.

Oliver didn't let them finish. "Remember, we were going to help Ms. Sandra at the church?"

Herman's smile disappeared. "Oh, okay."

"Thanks for the yarn, Herman!" Hyacinth called as Oliver dragged her and Laney by the hand to the church.

When Herman had biked out of sight, Oliver stopped and let go of his sisters' hands. "Oh good, he's gone." He spun on his heel and headed back to the garden.

"You lied to him!" Hyacinth said, running up next to Oliver. "He could have helped with the garden."

"That guy?" Oliver said. "Herman knocked me over with his bike the other day!"

"He didn't mean to!" Hyacinth said. "Anyways, I like him."

Oliver located the lock and spun the combination. "I can't believe you're defending him. You're not in his class. You don't know what he's really like. He talks about his money all the time. He's a showoff." He pushed the gate open.

"He's nice to me," Hyacinth said, carefully setting her new stash of yarn on a soil bag. "And the next time we see him, we should invite him to help with the garden."

"I doubt he'd want to. He's the kind of guy who won't want to get his hands dirty." Oliver waited for her to agree with him. But Hyacinth puffed out her cheeks, walked to the other side of the lot, and started yanking weeds with a vengeance.

✳ ✳ ✳

Jessie had given Laney a very important job: moving bricks from the back corner of the lot to the front. The bricks were heavy, but Laney had big muscles, so it wasn't a problem for her. She thought about how the bricks could be made into a path, just like in *The Wizard of Oz*. She wondered if the path would lead to a wizard's palace, where he could grant any wish she wanted.

She picked up a brick, thinking what she would wish for. A flying car, so they could go to that orchestra camp and bring Isa back home? Another bunny, so Paganini would have a friend? A counterspell, so Mama would bake double-chocolate pecan cookies again? Laney carried the brick slowly to the front of the lot, left it in the big pile, and went back to get another one. She was so lost in thought that she didn't realize she was almost done. There was only one brick left.

She picked it up. *If I think of a wish before I drop this brick off, my wish will come true*, Laney told herself. She got to the front of the lot and squeezed her eyes shut. *I wish Mr. Jeet would get healthy soon so he could come here and sit in the garden with me*, she wished with all her heart. Then she put the brick down by the fence where the soil was piled up. Hyacinth and Franz came over, and Hyacinth climbed up on the mountain of soil bags and sighed.

"What's wrong?" Laney asked. Now that she was done with the bricks, she could go back to digging for rocks.

"Nothing's wrong," Hyacinth said, taking out her knitting. Franz collapsed on the ground, exhausted.

"Okay," Laney said. "Want to help me look for a blue rock?" She used her trowel to dig. She had always wanted a blue rock.

"I don't think there are any blue rocks here," Hyacinth said, winding her yarn around her fingers.

"I bet there are," Laney said. Her trowel hit

something hard, and she brushed away the dirt. It wasn't a rock, but as she dug it out, the leaves overhead rustled as if they were saying, *Hurry, Laney! There's treasure in there, Laney!* It took some work, but finally she pulled out a small wooden box. "Look!" she called to Hyacinth.

Her sister joined her. Laney held up the box and brushed away the dirt. There was a little metal latch, and she tried to pry it open.

"What are you looking at?" Oliver and Jessie asked, walking over to them. They had dirt streaks across their arms and faces.

"Buried treasure!" Laney exclaimed. "But it won't open."

Jessie put her hand out. "Let me try."

Laney passed it over, and Jessie pried the metal piece with her fingernail. The hinge rotated and released.

"Let me open it!" Laney said, grabbing for the box.

"Be careful," Hyacinth warned. "It might be dangerous."

Laney lifted the lid and found a disintegrating folded piece of paper. And inside the lid, etched into the wood, was "Luciana."

"Could that be—" began Oliver.

"No, it's impossible," Jessie interrupted him.

"But it might have been . . ." Hyacinth started.

They stared at the box.

"It looks like it was buried a *long* time ago," Jessie said, examining it.

"Mr. Beiderman told me and Hyacinth that she liked to hide and bury things," Laney said.

"Wait, let me think," Jessie said. She stared at the sky, calculating something in her head. "This used to be a preschool, and Luciana would have been the right age to go to school here before it closed down," Jessie noted. "But that doesn't mean this box was hers."

"Mr. Beiderman always has a funny reaction when we talk about the church," Oliver said. "Remember when I mentioned it in the basement the other day and he left so fast?"

"I'm going to give it to him," Laney announced.

"No!" Jessie, Oliver, and Hyacinth said.

"What if it's not his Luciana?" Jessie said.

"And what if it is?" Oliver added. "That might be worse."

"It would give him sad memories," Jessie finished.

For a moment, the only sound was the wind tossing the Silver Queen's leaves. Did Luciana collect the leaves and make crowns for her head? Did the Silver Queen remember Luciana? Hyacinth spent a moment observing the way the leaves swayed as if whispering an ancient secret.

"I think this is Mr. Beiderman's Luciana," Hyacinth finally said, breaking the silence. "And look." She reached into the box and gently removed the crumbling brown piece of paper. "These are seeds. She wants this garden as much as we do."

Nineteen

That afternoon when the kids went home for lunch, they found Papa lying on the couch reading a book about a computer genius, resting his still-strained back. They scarfed down their lunch, eager to return to the garden, knowing that Orlando, Angie, and Benjamin would be waiting for them at the gate to help spread the soil.

"Where are you off to now?" Papa asked as he watched them put on their shoes, laying his book on his chest.

"Oh, the playground," Jessie said vaguely.

"Again? If you want, you can stick around here and we can play board games," he said, his eyes hopeful.

The Vanderbeeker kids exchanged glances.

"We, uh, promised some kids we'd play basketball with them," Oliver said. "I need to keep up for next season."

Papa's face fell. "Okay. Have fun." He sighed and picked up his book.

"I love you, Papa," Laney said, giving him a kiss.

"If your mom were here, she'd say, 'Be careful!'"

"We're always careful," Oliver said.

* * *

When they arrived at the garden, Oliver let them in, and the sounds of squeaky bus brakes and wailing ambulance sirens were instantly muffled by the walls covered with ivy. A chorus of birdsong welcomed the kids, the tree leaves rustled hello, and two squirrels did a spiral race up the Silver Queen and chattered at the Vanderbeekers from a high branch.

Laney and Oliver beelined for the bags of soil and climbed to the top.

"Be careful!" Jessie said. Laney waved at her.

They slid down the bags, Oliver tumbling dramatically off the pile and Laney narrowly avoiding getting her brand-new front teeth knocked out as Jessie stepped in and caught her before she face-planted on the ground.

A slight rattle of the garden gate interrupted them. Oliver ran over and loud-whispered, "What's the secret password?"

"You didn't give us one, goofball." It was Angie's voice, so Oliver opened the gate.

"Whoa," Angie said, stepping inside with Orlando and Benjamin behind her. "You guys did a lot. It looks really . . . empty in here."

"Is this the soil you want us to help move?" Orlando asked him.

Benjamin rolled his head from side to side and shook out his arms. "We carry heavy things," he said in his best Neanderthal impression.

Orlando side-eyed him, then looked at the Vanderbeekers. "What's the plan?"

Jessie, Oliver, Orlando, and Benjamin got themselves organized in a human chain. The first person—Orlando—would pick up a bag of soil and hand it to Jessie, who would hand it off to Benjamin, who would hand it to Oliver. After passing it, Orlando would run past everyone to join the line after Oliver, and the others would run to the front of the line after they passed it on, so the soil would continue moving across the lot until it traveled to the opposite end. Hyacinth was in charge of cutting open the bag with the craft scissors she kept in her knitting pouch. Then she and Laney would drag the soil around, distributing it over the lot.

The soil mountain got smaller and smaller, until there were only six bags left. They used three of those to fill the toilet and bathtub with soil, because why not? They saved the last few bags to put in and around the hole they dug for Tilia next to the Silver Queen. Orlando carefully lifted Tilia out of her pot and set her in her new home, and they packed the good soil around her root ball.

Hyacinth and Laney cheered, and then everyone collapsed on the ground, their arms like limp noodles.

They stared up at the rectangle of blue sky and breathed in the fresh soil smell. Hyacinth couldn't believe she'd once thought this place was haunted. It was definitely *alive*, but in a good, cheerful way, with birds fluttering and chirping, squirrels scurrying and chattering. The Silver Queen was the guardian of the garden, standing proud and waving hello whenever the kids entered through the gate.

Hyacinth looked up and up and up into the sky and wondered how far she was looking. Was it twenty miles? Less than that? More? The soil was cool against her back, and she lost herself in the pretty blue and the sounds of birds singing and leaves whispering in the breeze. The garden was alive all around them, Hyacinth thought, and soon Luciana's seeds would be part of it.

Off to the side, Oliver cracked a joke and the air filled with laughter. Hyacinth breathed in the happiness, her heart filling with the sounds of a hundred trumpets, a hundred celebratory horns.

❁ ❁ ❁

Jessie looked out at the transformed land, then realized that there was a *lot* of space to fill. How were they going to make this into a garden in just two weeks? Where would they find the money?

As her worries grew, Orlando came up and lightly punched her shoulder. "Hey," he said. "This looks awesome."

"It does, doesn't it?" Jessie said. Everyone gathered around. "Now that the soil is ready, what are we going to do about getting plants and flowers?"

"My dad keeps buying plants and then not taking care of them," Angie said. "I've had to take over all the watering and pruning. I'll ask if I can bring some of them here."

"Can indoor plants survive outdoors?" asked Hyacinth.

"It depends," Orlando said.

Jessie tapped her finger on her temple, thinking. "Would it be weird to have a collection of abandoned houseplants? That wouldn't really fit in with the . . . ah, theme of the garden."

"What theme?" Oliver said to Jessie. "A garden is a garden. Plants go in a garden. Who cares what they are?"

"Mr. Jeet will care," Hyacinth said. "And Miss Josie. You know how careful she is about her plants. Some need light; others don't. Some she waters every day; some only once a week."

"This is getting so complicated," Oliver said, rubbing his eyes.

Jessie sighed. "I guess we don't really have a choice. What we get is what we get, right? We can't be choosy; it's not like we have unlimited money to buy all the plants at Hiba's store and make this place look like the New York Botanical Garden."

"We have Luciana's seeds," Laney chimed in. "There are lots of 'em."

"Hey, y'all, I know where we could get great plants," Orlando said, breaking the silence.

The Vanderbeekers looked back at him and realized at once what he was talking about. Of course!

Jessie looked up at the darkening sky. "That will be a perfect project for tomorrow," she said. She headed to the gate, opening it an inch to check that it was safe to leave without being detected, then opened it wide to let everyone out. Oliver locked the gate behind them.

The Vanderbeekers and Angie were saying goodbye to Benjamin and Orlando when Mr. Smiley came around the corner holding a pizza box.

"I've got dinner, Angie," he called.

"Pizza!" Angie cried.

Mr. Smiley smiled at everyone; then his eyes drifted to the overflowing trash can by the curb. He pointed to the labels on the empty bags of soil. "That's the same type of soil that's in our courtyard," he observed.

There was silence; then Angie spoke up.

"Um, Dad? That *is* the soil that was in our courtyard."

The look on Mr. Smiley's face told everyone that they were in big, *big* trouble.

❖ ❖ ❖

The Vanderbeeker kids were huddled in Jessie and Isa's bedroom, trying to hear what Mr. Smiley was saying to Mama and Papa.

"There's no yelling. That's a good sign," Oliver observed.

No one answered him. Finally, they heard Mama call them downstairs. A very annoyed-looking Mr. Smiley was standing by the front door.

"We can explain," Oliver began, thinking it would be best to start talking first.

Mama's eyebrows arched. "You can explain why you stole eighty-four bags of soil from Mr. Smiley?"

Oliver gulped. "'Stole' is such a strong word."

"Did you ask for his permission?" Papa asked.

Jessie, Oliver, and Hyacinth didn't respond, so Laney said, "Nope!"

"Did you pay him for the soil?" Mama asked as she crossed her arms.

"Nope!" Laney answered again. "Well, I don't think we did." She looked at her siblings. "Did we?"

Oliver sighed. "No, we did not. Okay, I see what you're getting at."

"Unfortunately, you cannot return the soil to him," Papa said. "Angie said you put all that soil in the park."

Oliver swallowed. The soil wasn't *technically* in a park, but he wasn't about to rat Angie out.

"It was nice of you to think about making the park beautiful, but the Parks Department should be taking care of that. Thankfully, Mr. Smiley has thought up a very generous arrangement for you," Papa continued. "He's letting Angie work off the cost of the soil, and he thought he would let you do that too."

"Really?" the kids asked.

"You will sort all his building's recycling for the rest of the summer," Papa informed them.

The rest of the summer? Oliver thought. *Isn't that a bit harsh?*

"I think Mr. Smiley is being very generous," Mama continued.

"There's backlog in the basement, and it needs to be sorted by Thursday before the Department of Sanitation picks it up," Mr. Smiley said.

The Vanderbeeker kids nodded bravely.

Oliver cleared his throat and tried to flash his most charming smile. "Sounds great, Mr. Smiley. And we're really sorry about taking all your soil."

"Angie will meet you at eight tomorrow morning," Mr. Smiley said.

He did not smile back.

SUNDAY, JULY 1

Days Mr. Jeet in Hospital: 6

Days Until Garden
Extravaganza: 13

Twenty

Angie was waiting for the Vanderbeekers in front of her building the next morning when they arrived for recycling duty.

"I'm sorry I got you guys in trouble," Angie said. "I told Dad it was all my fault, but he wouldn't listen to me. You guys can be off the hook if you want."

The Vanderbeekers shook their heads.

"We had a part in it too," Oliver said.

"I should have listened to my instincts," Jessie said. "There's a scientific basis for instinctual reactions, you know."

"We better get started," Angie said. "There's so much to do." She led them into the basement.

Laney was the first to see the pile of trash bags. They reached up to the ceiling!

"Wow!" Laney said. "Your building has *so* much more trash than ours!"

Angie smiled grimly. "That's not the trash. That's the recycling we need to sort."

Oliver groaned. "Your dad said there were only a few bags! Is it too late to blame all this on you?"

"Yes," replied Angie. She opened the first bag. A horrible smell greeted them, and everyone took a big step backward.

"Eww!" Laney said, holding her nose.

"That's awful!" Jessie said. "I thought people were supposed to rinse their recyclables."

Angie nodded. "You would think, especially since Dad puts big posters from the Department of Sanitation on each floor. But—nope."

Jessie looked sick as she pulled out a Styrofoam takeout container with food still inside it. "I'm trying not to lose my faith in humanity," she said.

"Styrofoam can't be recycled," Angie said. "Just throw it in here." She pulled over the trash can nearest to them.

Jessie threw it inside, then gagged.

"Are you going to throw up?" Laney asked.

"Turn away from me if you are," Oliver said. "These are my favorite sneakers."

Jessie, Hyacinth, and Laney continued to pick through the bag while Oliver and Angie grabbed another one. They silently went through the contents, throwing away some things, setting some items aside to get rinsed in the utility sink, and sorting the clean recyclables into separate bins Mr. Smiley had left for them.

Pretty soon Jessie's team was done with their first bag, and they opened another.

"Whoa, look!" Laney said. She pulled out containers of paint jugs.

"Oh good, they're clean." Jessie sighed with relief. "Put them in that big blue bin," she instructed Laney.

Laney didn't listen to her. "Look, if you turn it on its side, it looks like a pig! See, there's the nose and snout!"

Hyacinth joined in. "You can draw in eyes right there." She pointed. "And a mouth."

Jessie huffed. "Can we please get moving?" She moved on to the next bag and opened it. This time there was no decaying food, but mixed in with the recyclables were hundreds of foam peanuts.

"Oh no," Angie said. "Those foam things need to be separated and thrown away, and they are a Pain. In. The. Butt. They get staticky and stick to everything."

"Ugh!" the Vanderbeekers said all at once.

Mr. Smiley sure was making them sorry for ever having touched that soil.

❊ ❊ ❊

When nine o'clock rolled around, Angie took off to visit her Aunt Ursula with her dad ("I hope I don't smell too bad!" she said), and the Vanderbeekers left the basement and went upstairs and out of the building. After securing permission from Mr. Smiley, they took a few items with them: two tires, all the empty paint jugs, two paint buckets, a set of old speakers, and a three-foot-long plank of wood. Hyacinth and Laney persuaded Oliver and Jessie to carry it all up with them.

"Oh, sweet, fresh air," Oliver said, taking big gulps of air while resting the tire he had just brought upstairs against the building.

"I need a shower," Jessie said, dragging up the second tire and a bag of paint jugs. She leaned into Oliver. "Do I smell?"

"Of course you smell," Oliver said, moving away. "We all do."

Franz, who had heard their voices from outside the brownstone, shoved his face against the living room window and howled. Drool dribbled down the glass. George Washington, who was napping on the windowsill, jumped up in alarm and scrambled out of sight.

"Oh, sweetie!" Hyacinth said, touching the glass. "How's the best dog in the world doing?"

"I don't want to shower now if I have to shower later," Laney said, a bunch of foam peanuts stuck to her hair.

"I'm fine with that," Oliver said.

Jessie smelled her shirt and winced, but she reluctantly agreed. "Let's go."

"Wait!" Oliver said. "We forgot Miss Josie's seedlings!"

"Right!" Jessie said, then paused, remembering the soil disaster. "But let's ask her first." Jessie took out her phone and called Miss Josie.

"Hi, Miss Josie," Jessie said, clicking her phone to speaker.

"Hi, Miss Josie!" Laney, Hyacinth, and Oliver chorused.

Miss Josie's warm, amber voice came through the speaker. "Hello, my dear ones."

"How's Mr. Jeet?" Oliver asked.

"He's on the mend," Miss Josie said. "He's napping; otherwise I'd let you speak to him."

Laney leaned into the speaker and yelled, "When are you coming home? Paganini misses you!"

"Laney, geez, indoor voice," Jessie said.

Miss Josie's laugh filled their ears. "Oh, how I've missed you. I don't know when we'll be home. He has a long recovery ahead."

"Can you make sure he's back by July thirteenth?" Oliver asked, and Jessie jabbed him in the ribs. "Ouch!"

"What did you say, honey?" Miss Josie asked.

"He said to make sure Mr. Jeet eats lots of protein," Jessie said, glaring at her brother. "Anyways, we're calling because you know those seedlings you've been growing? We've been watering them for you, and they look like they're ready to get planted. Do you want us to do that?"

"Oh goodness, I had completely forgotten about those! Yes, please plant them wherever you want. I usually keep some for my windowsill, but feel free to give the rest away. Will you distribute them for me?"

"Of course, Miss Josie! You can trust us!" Jessie said before saying goodbye and hanging up.

The Vanderbeekers did a communal fist bump, and Jessie, Oliver, and Laney started up the stairs.

"I'll meet you back here," Hyacinth said. "I'm going to pick up Franz and get my knitting." Hyacinth dashed into their apartment while her siblings headed upstairs to get the seedling trays. She emerged outside just as Oliver finished loading the wagon with Hyacinth's and Laney's recycled finds. The sisters each carried a tray overflowing with vibrant green shoots and leaves.

"Be careful!" Jessie screeched as Laney jumped down the last two brownstone steps, jostling the tray.

"I *am* being careful!" Laney huffed. "I'm treating these plants like my little babies!"

Slowly they made their way down the street, avoiding the sidewalk bumps where tree roots had pushed up against the concrete. A figure was sitting on the steps of the church, and when the Vanderbeekers got closer, they saw that it was Herman Huxley. He was knitting.

"Hi, Herman!" Hyacinth said.

"You're here *again?*" Oliver said, in a voice Hyacinth thought did not sound much like her brother's at all.

Herman didn't say anything back, but his fingers tightened around the knitting needles.

Hyacinth, however, collected her bravery and stood face-to-face with Oliver. "Stop being mean," she demanded.

For a moment, Oliver looked stunned. Then he glared at her. Then he crossed his arms. "I'm not being mean. *He* is." He pointed a finger at Herman.

There was a long pause before Herman spoke up.

"It's okay," he said to Hyacinth. "I guess I haven't always been the nicest person to your brother."

Hyacinth gaped. "*You're* mean to *Oliver?*" She couldn't imagine anyone being mean to her brother.

Herman picked up his yarn bag and hung it over his bike handles. "I'll go."

"No, Herman, stay!" Hyacinth called out, but he was already on his way. A few seconds later, he disappeared around the corner.

Hyacinth squinted at Oliver. "See what you did?"

"What?" Oliver said, confused. He looked at Jessie. "What did I do?"

"You are sort of being . . . mean," Jessie said.

"You don't like him either!" Oliver defended himself. "And don't forget who his father is."

Hyacinth shook her head and walked to the garden gate to open the combination lock. "The next time I see him, I'm inviting him to help us with the garden."

Oliver rolled his eyes. "He's not going to want to help."

Hyacinth spun around and stared at Oliver with challenge in her eyes. "I bet you a million dollars he will."

❖ ❖ ❖

They spent the rest of the day transplanting Miss Josie's seedlings and putting Luciana's seeds into the ground. Laney wanted the seeds to be planted in the very center of the garden, which required the precise measuring of footsteps to determine the exact right spot. Oliver and Laney used the bricks to create a circular planter, using a large Hula-Hoop as their guide. Inside the circle, they sprinkled Luciana's seeds and Laney sang a welcome song to them.

Hyacinth was quiet all afternoon and on the way home for dinner. Oliver knew she was disappointed with him, and he didn't like not living up to Hyacinth's standards. It bothered him so much that the second he was excused from dinner, he asked if he could go to the basketball courts.

"Be back in one hour," Mama said.

Oliver stuck his feet into his sneakers, grabbed his basketball, and left without saying a word. The second he got outside, he saw Angie sitting on the stoop two doors down.

"Hey," Angie said. "Are you going to the courts?"

"Yeah," Oliver said, dribbling the basketball with angry thuds.

Angie joined him as he walked. Halfway down the block, she spoke. "How was the gardening today?"

"It sucked. Herman was there, being annoying and

showing off again. I thought you were going to come later."

"I went with my dad to visit my Aunt Ursula today. Remember? I told you."

Oliver took a deep breath to calm himself. "We planted Miss Josie's seedlings in the garden. Want to see?"

"Sure!"

When they arrived at the garden, Oliver found that the ivy he had carefully used to cover up the lock had been ripped away from the gate and lay in withered pieces on the ground. The fence where the lock had been attached was twisted and broken, the lock nowhere to be seen.

"Hey! What happened?" Oliver exclaimed.

"Shh!" Angie whispered. "It could be a robber! He could still be in there!"

"Why would a robber want to get in here? There's nothing to steal," Oliver said, but he opened the gate as quietly as he could. They peeked inside.

The trees didn't wave to him. The ivy didn't flutter. The birds were silent.

Oliver pushed the gate open wider. "What are all

those pink flags doing here?" He walked over to where they had carefully planted the herb seedlings.

Angie gasped. "Your poor plants!"

Oliver leaned down to take a closer look; many had been stepped on. He tried to lift them up, but they just withered back to the ground.

"Wait," Angie said. "Don't disturb the footprints. They're clues." She leaned closer to examine them, then stood up and looked at Oliver. "Do we know anyone who wears fancy shoes with no tread?"

✷ ✷ ✷

Oliver and Angie raced back to the brownstone to tell Jessie, Hyacinth, and Laney what had happened. The girls all wanted to go to the garden immediately to see the damage for themselves, but Mama enforced their curfew.

"It's eight o'clock," Mama told them. "Where would you want to go at this hour?"

Because no one could answer that question, the kids slunk back upstairs to get ready for bed.

They slept fitfully. Laney kept getting up and

visiting her siblings, asking them if they knew what time it was. Oliver tried to get himself sleepy by counting the books on his bookshelves. He had two hundred and sixty-one, and even after he counted them all, he still wasn't tired. Jessie recited the periodic table over and over again by memory, and Hyacinth slept in her sleeping bag on the floor so she could snuggle with Franz. It felt as if morning would never come.

Monday, July 2

Days Mr. Jeet in Hospital: 7

Days Until Garden
Extravaganza: 12

Twenty-One

At five minutes to eight, the kids rushed to Angie's building to go through the recycling.

"I wish I could go with you to the garden," Angie said once nine o'clock rolled around.

"Your dad wouldn't be happy if you cut class," Oliver said. "He'd probably give us another year of recycling duty."

"I like recycling duty!" Laney said. She had found lots of egg cartons she wanted to use as seed starters.

"Tell me everything this afternoon," Angie made them promise. "And remember, analyze the footprints!" she called as she raced down the street.

The Vanderbeekers ran to the garden, and when

they pushed open the gate, Hyacinth shielded her eyes. "I'm too afraid to look!" she said.

"Oh, this looks bad," Jessie said.

The dirt was kicked up in different areas, and the little pink flags were everywhere. Dozens of seedlings were trampled.

"Look at the footprints," Oliver said. "See how this one has a smooth sole? It's exactly like my dress shoes are—no tread. And over here—that's definitely a construction boot." The imprint was full of symmetrical rectangular squares, unlike the scattered tread of their sneakers.

Hyacinth set her foot on top of one of the footprints. "These are huge!" she said.

Jessie's face was grim. "I know exactly who did this. We've got to call Triple J." She pulled out her phone and dialed. Again the call went unanswered, and Jessie left another call-me-back-right-away message.

"Something fishy is definitely going on," Jessie said. "Where is Triple J? And why isn't he answering his phone?"

"We need to go to the source," Oliver said. "Right now."

* * *

Hyacinth didn't understand why they had to go to Mr. Huxley's house. Couldn't they just call him? He probably wasn't even home! But Oliver insisted they needed to confront him in person because it was too easy to lie to someone on the phone.

Hyacinth didn't like confrontation. She liked it when everyone got along and was happy and nice to one another. But Oliver was a man with a mission, and he wasn't going to stop until he had answers.

Even though Oliver had never been to Herman's place, everyone knew where he lived because it was on the same block as their school *and* because Herman always boasted about living in the newest luxury building in Harlem.

Hyacinth followed her siblings to Adam Clayton Powell Jr. Boulevard, then north to 144th Street. Oliver stopped in front of a shiny silver condo building with floor-to-ceiling windows on every story.

"That's his building, but I don't know which apartment he lives in," Oliver told them when they arrived. "Maybe his name is on the buzzer." He started scanning the names on the electronic keypad, shading the top of the console to make it easier to see the digital monitor.

"Hey, Oliver?" said Hyacinth.

"Yeah?"

"I think I know what floor he lives on." Hyacinth pointed.

Each floor had a balcony, but the fifth-floor balcony was the one that stood out. The railings were wrapped in multicolored yarn, and long finger-knit garlands draped over them in perfect waves. The balcony looked as if a stack of rainbow sweaters had exploded all over it.

"Holy smokes," Jessie said. "Hyacinth, you have officially met your match."

Oliver found "5" on the console and pressed it. The front door buzzed. Oliver pushed the door open and led his sisters up the stairs to the fifth floor. Hyacinth lagged far behind, wondering if she could go back downstairs and wait outside on the sidewalk. She didn't want any part of this confrontation. Before she could ask Jessie if that would be okay, the door on the fifth floor opened.

"What are you doing here?" Herman asked, surprise on his face. "I thought you were the grocery delivery."

"You get your *groceries* delivered to your *apartment?*" asked Laney.

Herman frowned. "My dad's too busy to go to the store."

"He's too busy to buy *food?*" Laney said, befuddled.

Herman ignored her. "What do you want?"

Oliver spoke up, his voice belligerent. "We came to see your dad. We want to know what he's doing to our garden."

"My dad is at work. And I doubt he was in your garden."

"He stomped all over Miss Josie's seedlings, which she grew from scratch! And he put up tons of pink flags everywhere!" Oliver said.

"Wait a second," Herman said, holding up a hand. "He put flags in your backyard?"

"No, in the garden we're working on next to the church."

"I knew you were up to something over there," Herman said.

"Did he do it or not?" Oliver demanded.

Hyacinth stepped in front of Oliver and looked at Herman. "Do you want to see it? The garden?"

There was a long pause.

Then a big grin took over Herman's face.

Hyacinth smiled back and looked at Oliver. "You owe me a million dollars."

✦ ✦ ✦

It was a quick trip back to the church. There was no lock to the garden anymore, so the kids pushed open the gate and stepped right in. The pink flags were still there.

Oliver pointed at the pink flags. "See those? We heard your dad talking to developers about selling the land, and the next thing we know, there are pink flags everywhere and a bunch of Miss Josie's seedlings were trampled. My uncle works in construction, and he uses pink flags to mark surveying areas. White would be for excavation spots, yellow for gas lines, orange for telecommunications—"

"Okay," Jessie interrupted. "We get it."

Herman hesitated, then spoke. "I heard my dad

talking to someone on the phone at dinner the other night. He said something about land by the church—"

"That's this place!" Laney cried.

"—and how they could sell it to a condominium developer."

"What's a cond-min-um?" Laney asked.

"It's a boring building," Jessie said, "that's going to be built right on top of our perfect garden."

Herman ran his hands through his hair. "I'm sorry," he said. He walked over to a pink flag and pulled it out. "But maybe it won't happen. Land deals fall through all the time."

"Are you allowed to take those out?" Hyacinth asked, her fingers pulling at the hem of her shirt.

Herman yanked another flag out of the garden. "Do you want a building here or not?"

Twenty-Two

Pretty soon all the Vanderbeekers were helping Herman. They were careful not to step on the seedlings, and soon enough they had plucked all the flags from the soil. Laney collected them to stick in their backyard when they returned home; she thought they looked pretty.

"Is it really worth working here anymore?" Oliver said. "If it's all just going to be bulldozed?"

The others looked back at him, then out at the garden. They thought of all the dreams they had for the space. Jessie could practically see Mr. Jeet and Miss Josie sitting on a bench, surrounded by plants and chatting with their friends and neighbors. Oliver could imagine racing up the Silver Queen with Angie and Jimmy L, hiding himself among the summer leaves. Hyacinth was envisioning a lazy Sunday afternoon after church, sitting next to Tilia of the Eternal Spring with Mr. Beiderman and Franz. And Laney thought about all the herbs and vegetables they could grow for Paganini. Why, they could grow enough for a dozen bunnies!

At the same time, it hurt to look out at the space and all that possibility—the seedlings; Luciana's seeds; and the Silver Queen, which had shown Hyacinth the way into the garden in the first place. Would all their dreams and hard work be destroyed by a cookie-cutter condominium complex?

⚙ ⚙ ⚙

Jessie asked her siblings to be ready to vote that night: Should they or should they not continue working on the garden? When they arrived home, Oliver took refuge in his bedroom to think about it. Was it worth putting more work into the garden when it would most likely be destroyed?

Oliver didn't think so. He was going to vote no.

The doorbell interrupted his thoughts, but he didn't

have the energy to race downstairs to answer it. He heard the door open, then Jessie's voice, then Orlando's. A moment later, their chatter faded away.

It was the perfect time to look for much-needed candy in Jessie and Isa's room. He slipped into the hallway and then into the twins' bedroom, undetected.

He started with the usual places. He pulled up Jessie's mattress, looked under the bed, and yanked up the loose floorboard. Nothing. She had probably changed her hiding place after the last time he'd gotten into her jelly-bean stash. He poked around on her messy desk. Then he opened her desk drawers, starting at the top. Two drawers down, he heard a familiar crinkle.

Jackpot! A whole unopened bag of mini-Snickers! Oliver picked up the bag—he might as well take it all—but underneath it, a letter caught his eye. Along the top it read "PECKS POND SCIENCE CAMP," with "Congratulations!" below Jessie's name.

Oliver was confused. This was the science camp Jessie had been talking about all year—the one she *hadn't* gotten into. He pulled out the letter and sat on her desk chair to read it.

Pecks Pond Science Camp

Dear Jessie,

Congratulations! You have been chosen to participate in this year's science camp! We received hundreds of applicants but could choose only fifty. We were very impressed by your science fair project, "Endothermic and Exothermic Reactions."

We are happy to provide you with a full-tuition scholarship, although due to funding restrictions, we cannot provide any financial assistance with room and board or transportation. Scholars who require further financial assistance are encouraged to apply for individual grants.

We look forward to meeting you in August! Please have a parent or guardian sign the enclosed release forms and send them back to us with a $200 deposit for room and board. The remainder of the fee is due no later than May 1.

If your plans have changed and you are no longer able to attend, please let us know so we can accept applicants from the wait list.

Sincerely,
Tisha Hernandez
Director, Pecks Pond Science Camp

Oliver put the letter down. So Jessie *had* gotten into science camp after all. His mind reeled. Why hadn't she gone? He read the letter again, and one sentence stood out: ". . . we cannot provide any financial assistance with room and board or transportation." Did Jessie say no because she knew their parents were already paying those expenses for Isa's orchestra camp? And did she say she hadn't gotten in so Isa and her parents wouldn't feel bad?

It was amazing how generous people could be without wanting or expecting something in return. He knew how much Jessie had wanted to go to science camp; it was all she'd talked about for months. Maybe, Oliver thought, maybe the world worked only if people gave all they could without measuring the worth of what they gave.

He went downstairs to find Jessie. He was surprised to see everyone in the basement, sitting on the floor. Hyacinth and Herman were knitting; Orlando was using a Swiss Army knife to cut into jugs that looked suspiciously like the paint jugs they had sorted during their recycling duties. Angie and Laney were painting the jugs, and Jessie was sketching a complicated diagram with lots of arrows in her science notebook.

"We need to go ahead with the garden," Oliver said in a rush. "We have to do it for Mr. Jeet and Miss Josie, and for the whole neighborhood. The garden is perfect, and we need to save it and share it with everyone. Even if it does get destroyed in fourteen days." He watched everyone exchange glances. "What?" he demanded.

"We've been waiting for you," said Hyacinth.

"Yeah, come on. We need your help making these into planters," Orlando added, motioning toward the jugs.

"Wait, you all decided to go ahead? Even though it might get destroyed?" Oliver said.

"Get with the program, Oliver," Jessie said. "We have so much to do before the Garden Extravaganza!"

MONDAY, JULY 9

Days Mr. Jeet in Hospital: 14

Days Until Garden
Extravaganza: 5

Twenty-Three

A week flew past. By the following Monday, they had made lots of progress on the garden. Herman had donated his bike lock, an eighteen-millimeter-thick gold-standard-rated padlock, to keep the gate secured so that if the building developers came back, they couldn't get inside and mess up all the new plants. Laney checked Luciana's seeds every day, but there were no signs of growth. Herman had an iPod, so they loaded Vivaldi's *Four Seasons* on it and set it on the brick circle to play music in hopes it would encourage the seeds to emerge.

Hyacinth and Herman spent time sanding down the long plank of wood they'd found in Mr. Smiley's basement, which they placed on top of two plastic paint buckets to make a bench. They wrapped the board in a few layers of rainbow knitting to make it softer for Mr. Jeet and Miss Josie to sit on, then put the finished bench under the Silver Queen.

Every time Angie came to the garden, she brought some of her dad's abandoned houseplants. They planted them all in the southwest quadrant of the garden, with Miss Josie's seedlings. Oliver discovered a spigot on the side of the church, and they spent many hours filling the watering cans and trying to keep the plants from perishing in the hot weather.

During the week, they talked about anything and everything while they worked, with the exception of one topic: Mr. Jeet. He had moved out of the Intensive Care Unit into a general care wing, but there was still no word on when he would come home.

Five days before the Garden Extravaganza—four days before Isa was due home—the Vanderbeekers and Herman were working in the garden when Orlando burst in and demanded that they all follow him. He led them all the way across Harlem to the Madison Avenue Bridge on East 138th Street and crossed over to the South Bronx. Right over the bridge was a gated area with a huge painted sign that said LA FINCA DEL SUR COMMUNITY GARDEN. Orlando went inside, where five people, all wearing floppy hats, were manning a table filled with plants in seedling trays. Beyond them were garden beds with plants spilling out in every direction.

"Plant sale!" one of the women said. "Ten dollars a flat!"

Jessie examined the trays and looked back at everyone. "Each flat holds forty-eight plants."

"You can mix and match," the woman told them. "We have squash, tomatoes, cukes, herbs, and flowers."

"This is a garden paradise," Laney breathed.

"Why are they so cheap?" Herman said with skepticism.

"We got a grant from the parks department," the woman told him. "We're all volunteers. Our goal is to get everyone growing in the South Bronx."

"What about Harlem?" Laney asked. "That's where we live."

"We'd love for you to start growing in Harlem too," she told them. "We want to make this whole city a garden!"

"Try some cherry tomatoes," said a woman with her hair in dozens of tiny braids that trailed down her back. She held out a basket.

Everyone took a few and popped them in their mouths. Oliver bit down on one, and it was like sunshine exploding in his mouth.

"Those taste amazing," Jessie told them.

The gardeners pointed to a basketball-player-tall guy who wore a straw hat and a beige tracksuit. The man tilted his hat and smiled at them. "That's the tomato guy," the gardeners said.

The Vanderbeekers and Herman and Orlando conferred.

"We have around thirty dollars left in our budget," Jessie told them. "Should we blow it all on these plants?"

The answer was a unanimous yes. Then Herman and Orlando kicked in another ten dollars each so they could buy two more trays. They picked three trays of assorted flowers: purple and pink petunias and daisies with sunshine-yellow centers; spring-green and lavender hostas and red geraniums; impatiens in a rainbow of colors; and something called Dusty Miller, which had leaves that looked like snowflakes.

The vegetables were harder to decide on. Jessie and Hyacinth didn't like cucumbers and refused to put them into the garden, but Orlando insisted they could make pickles with them. Hyacinth was skeptical that a vegetable as gross as cucumbers could turn into something as delicious as pickles. While everyone was arguing about the cucumbers, Laney filled an entire tray with plants Paganini would enjoy: red and green lettuce, kale, chard, basil, sage, and cilantro. They felt as if they had won the plant jackpot as they paid for the five trays.

"I want to live in your garden," Laney said.

The gardeners were so charmed by Laney that they gave her some seed packets so she could grow her own tricolored carrots. After thanking the gardeners, the Vanderbeekers, Orlando, and Herman trooped back over the bridge with their trays. They spent the rest of the afternoon arguing over the placement of each of the two hundred and forty plants, finally deciding to place the plants in four quadrants.

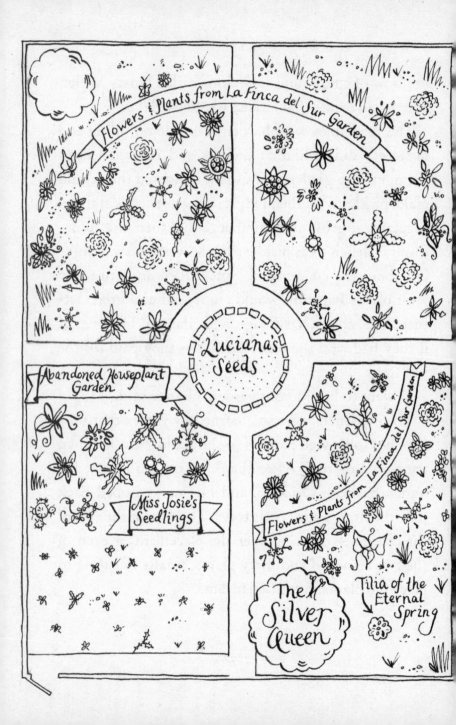

Flowers & Plants from La Finca del Sur Garden

Luciana's Seeds

Abandoned Houseplant Garden

Miss Josie's Seedlings

Flowers & Plants from La Finca del Sur Garden

The Silver Queen

Tilia of the Eternal Spring

"Too bad we couldn't have a lavender garden," Jessie said. "Mr. Beiderman would have liked that."

"Lavender was Luciana's favorite flower," Hyacinth told Herman.

"Uh-huh," he said.

"Mr. Jeet and Miss Josie are going to *love* this," Laney said. "It's going to be the best garden in the world!"

✿ ✿ ✿

Later that night, the Vanderbeekers gathered around the kitchen table for dinner. Before Papa sat down, he handed a few green M&M's he'd been saving to Laney, who stored them carefully in her skirt pocket. Then the kids looked at their mom for their daily report on Mr. Jeet.

"About the same," she reported as she passed out bowls of cold beet soup. Oliver was just getting up to add yet another check to the "Bad Days" column on the health chart when Laney pushed her bowl away from her. The red soup splashed onto the table, and Laney stood up on her chair.

"Laney!" Mama and Papa admonished at the exact same time.

"Get down right now! Where are your—" Mama started.

"I am going to the hospital tomorrow!" Laney announced, crossing her arms over her chest. She was tired of adults telling her what to do all the time. "Mr. Jeet needs me, and you can't stop me from visiting him."

Hyacinth stood up on her chair too. "I'm going too!"

Jessie stood up, although not on a chair, and joined her sisters in protest. "Me too."

Oliver, who was frozen by the chart, stared at his parents.

Mama and Papa looked up at the kids, then looked at each other.

"Mr. Jeet is not feeling well. He's still not talking," Mama warned them.

"I don't care!" Laney yelled.

"He's lost weight," Mama continued. "He has an IV needle in his arm and is hooked up to machines."

"We miss him. We want to see him," Jessie said, and Hyacinth nodded vigorously.

Mama did her silent-communication thing with Papa. That seemed to go on forever, until finally she nodded. "Okay. Tomorrow we'll all go see him."

"Hooray!" the kids shouted.

Laney, encouraged by this victory, pressed her luck. "And we demand regular food again! No more red soup! We want cookies!"

The lasers from Mama's eyes were enough to make Laney sit down hastily and pull her bowl toward her. Her siblings followed suit, sitting down in their chairs and bravely putting the soup into their mouths.

Despite the terrible beet soup, everyone was smiling.

TUESDAY, JULY 10

Days Mr. Jeet in Hospital: 15

Days Until Garden
Extravaganza: 4

Twenty-Four

Laney woke up and bounced out of bed. Today they would see Mr. Jeet! And she would bring Paganini. If anyone could cheer up Mr. Jeet, it was Paganini.

Laney considered her options. She couldn't bring Paganini in the pet carrier—too obvious! And her backpack was not that great a choice either. First of all, it had no air holes. Second, it was filled with stuff: two small bottles of hand sanitizer, a bag of mini-marsh-mallows (they made a good pillow *and* a great snack!), pictures her friends had drawn for her, pictures she had drawn for her friends but had forgotten to give to them before school ended, her inhaler just in case, and, at the very bottom, paper clips, hair ribbons, and a bunch of pencils with erasers shaped like hearts.

Laney searched her closet. Way at the back, under a stack of puzzles and board games, was a picnic basket. It was the perfect size; plus, it had little holes between the weavings, so Paganini could breathe. Laney would put some greens and rabbit pellets in there, and Paganini would be quite comfortable.

Laney knew it wasn't wise to tell anyone she was bringing Paganini; they would tell her not to because Paganini didn't have that therapy certificate everyone thought was so important.

When Laney went downstairs, she pursed her lips really, really tightly. She was not going to mention anything about Paganini! And pursing her lips paid off, because she didn't mention her bunny, not even once, and no one suspected *anything!* Even better, Oliver wasn't going to the hospital. He said he had important business with Mr. Beiderman that couldn't be delayed. That was good news, because her brother was the best at figuring out when people were hiding something.

So as Mama labeled food containers and placed a fresh batch of clothes for Miss Josie in a sturdy tote bag, Laney took greens from the fridge and stashed them in the basket along with a handful of rabbit pellets. When Mama announced that they were leaving in one minute, Laney quickly picked Paganini up in the picnic basket, then shut the flaps and hooked the latch so her rabbit couldn't pop out. A few seconds later, she could hear the faint sounds of Paganini chomping on the greens.

Mama led the way out of the brownstone. "Remember, girls. He's not talking, so don't ask him any questions," she reminded them. "Miss Josie is anxious enough; we don't want to make it worse."

The girls nodded solemnly, but Laney worried. If Mr. Jeet couldn't talk, then how would Laney figure out whether he liked having Paganini there?

They walked single file down 141st Street, then swung a right onto the main avenue. Soon the Vanderbeekers were marching through the hospital lobby. Hyacinth's yarn bag hung from her hips, and Jessie had a science encyclopedia under her arm because she needed to show Mr. Jeet an article about quarks. Laney carried the picnic basket carefully and smiled back at everyone who smiled at her; she didn't stop smiling, because then people might begin to suspect she had a bunny in her picnic basket. She didn't want to get all the way to the hospital only to be turned away at the last minute!

But sneaking Paganini into the hospital was easier than she thought. She had an adult with her, so no one would stop them because they were only kids. No one asked to check her basket. Mama led them into the elevator and punched the button for the fifth floor, a different floor from before, since Mr. Jeet had been moved out of Intensive Care a week ago. The elevator was crowded with people, including a man in a wheelchair who had tubes in his nose connected to something that looked like a bag filled with water on a rolling coat rack. He had two nurses with him: one who pushed the wheelchair and one who pushed the coat-rack thing.

At the back of the elevator was a man in a security uniform. Laney pulled her basket closer to her stomach. It was a good thing it was so crowded in there; she hoped the security guy didn't notice that the flaps of the basket were straining the latch, as if something was trying to get out. Laney put a hand on top of the basket. If Paganini got out, she would be in big trouble for sure.

She was relieved when Mama led the way out of the

crowded elevator onto the fifth floor. Right before the elevator fully closed, when the doors were only a sliver apart, she heard a man say "Did anyone else see something moving in that girl's basket?"

Laney thought she was caught, but Mama hadn't heard the man and was leading them down a hallway. Laney knew she needed to get to Mr. Jeet's room quick, in case the security guard came looking for her. Thankfully, the room was down only one hallway. Mama knocked on an open door that had the name Jeet written on a tag on the outside.

"Knock, knock!" Mama called.

"Come in!" Miss Josie's voice replied.

The three Vanderbeeker girls released a huge breath at the reassuring sound of their neighbor's voice. They peeked into the room, and there was Miss Josie, sitting in a brown plastic chair by the hospital bed, wearing one of her brightly colored dresses, which flowed down to her ankles. Then Laney turned her head, and there was Mr. Jeet! He was sitting up, and he didn't look like himself at all because he was wearing a gray hospital gown with tiny blue dots all over it instead of a button-down shirt and a bow tie.

Laney was so relieved to see him that she put the picnic basket down right on the hospital bed and climbed up next to him. She put her face two inches away from his and looked into his dark eyes. He still smelled like butterscotch candies. He put his right hand on her cheek, and Laney leaned in to give him a kiss. When she pulled away, she noticed tears in his eyes. Then she looked around and saw that Miss Josie was also crying, and Mama and Jessie and Hyacinth too!

Laney knew who could cheer everyone up. She put the picnic basket on her lap and flipped open the latch. Paganini popped his head up out of the basket, and Laney beamed a smile at everyone around her. But it was strange: no one looked happy to see Paganini! Mama looked horrified. Miss Josie looked stunned.

After a dazed moment of silence, Mr. Jeet began to laugh. He laughed so hard that more tears came from his eyes, but even Laney could tell they were happy tears. And the sound of his happiness suddenly made it worth all the trouble of bringing Paganini to the hospital.

"Holy cannoli!" Hyacinth blurted out when Paganini hopped out of the picnic basket and landed nimbly on Mr. Jeet's lap.

"Oh dear," Mama said, peeking outside at the nurses' station before closing the door to the room.

The sound of Mr. Jeet's laughter filled the air. "This is the first time he's laughed since the accident," Miss Josie said.

And Hyacinth had to admit that Mr. Jeet *did* look really happy. His mouth was crooked up on one side and his right hand was rubbing Paganini around the ears, the way Paganini liked best. Laney bounced on the bed in excitement.

"Laney, stop bouncing!" scolded Jessie.

Laney stopped, and Paganini stood up on his hind legs and snuffled at Mr. Jeet's chin. Laney rifled through the picnic basket and found some last pieces of food, then put the scraps into Mr. Jeet's right hand. Paganini immediately found them.

"Laney," Mama said, reaching for the rabbit, who

jumped just out of her reach. "We should probably put Paganini back. He's not allowed in the hospital."

"But Mama! Mr. Jeet loves Paganini! Look how happy he is!"

Hyacinth watched Mama's face and saw it soften as she looked at Paganini and Mr. Jeet. Her hands pulled back. "Well, maybe for just a few min—"

Before Mama could finish the sentence, the door burst open and a tall woman wearing a white lab coat and a stethoscope around her neck entered. "Hello, Mr. Jeet!" she boomed. "And how are you feeling to— Holy heck, is that a rabbit?"

Then Hyacinth heard heavy footsteps running toward the room from the hallway.

Hyacinth looked at Laney, who was trying to shove Paganini back into the picnic basket. But Paganini had other plans. He sprang out of Laney's hands and hopped onto the wheeled side table by Mr. Jeet's bed. There was a jug of ice water and a stack of plastic cups on top of it. Mama crouched down like a football player and tried to grab Paganini, but the velocity of his jump made the table swing out and she missed him by a few inches. As Paganini scrambled to regain his balance, he knocked over the water jug. The jug hit the floor, the top burst open, and water and ice splashed all over.

Then a man in a security uniform burst into the room yelling, "Is everything okay?" and promptly slipped on the water and ice. He went airborne for one second before falling smack on his back on the linoleum floor.

"Ouch!" Laney exclaimed.

"Are you okay, sir?" Miss Josie inquired, peering over the bed at him.

"Holy heck!" the doctor blurted out again.

Hyacinth picked up some ice from the floor and walked over to him. "Where does it hurt?"

"Everywhere," the man groaned.

Hyacinth put some ice cubes on his forehead, then piled some on his stomach just in case. Paganini scrambled off the table and back onto the bed, and Laney swiftly returned him to the picnic basket before she jumped down and helped Hyacinth gather more ice cubes for the injured security guard.

The doctor was not pleased. "This hospital has a very strict no-animal policy," she lectured Mama and Miss Josie. "Any that enter this medical facility must be certified therapy animals. Each one goes through an extensive training program here."

"We're so sorry," murmured Mama, while Miss Josie said, "Thank you for letting us know, dear."

"Stop with the ice," the man groaned from the floor. Laney ceased immediately, but Hyacinth had just gathered a big handful and didn't want to waste it, so she put it on his neck. She knew neck injuries could be very serious.

"Are you cold?" Hyacinth asked, concerned. She grabbed the blanket at the bottom of Mr. Jeet's bed and draped it across the man. "Don't worry. We're *really* great at making people feel better."

"That's quite right," Miss Josie said, leaning over to pat Hyacinth on the shoulder.

"Please leave me alone," the man said.

"I know who will make you feel better!" Laney said, reaching for the basket. "Paganini makes everyone feel better, right, Mr. Jeet?"

"No!" shouted Mama, Miss Josie, and Jessie. Mama yanked the basket away and put it down by her feet.

The right side of Mr. Jeet's mouth kicked up, and he waved his arm in the air.

"I'll walk you out," the doctor said to the Vanderbeekers. Her face was grim.

Miss Josie hugged Laney close. "I think your visit has been very good for Mr. Jeet."

"Even though we got in big trouble?" Laney whispered.

"It was worth it," Miss Josie whispered back.

WEDNESDAY, JULY 11

Days Mr. Jeet in Hospital: 16

Days Until Garden
Extravaganza: 3

Twenty-Five

Three days before the Garden Extravaganza, the Vanderbeekers walked to the garden to find the sidewalk in front of the gate filled with plants. There were two big pots of bright blue hydrangeas, four filled with peach-colored roses, a small tree with a scattering of green leaves, and twenty pots of lavender.

Laney ran to the tree and hugged it. Hyacinth leaned over to smell the roses. Jessie and Oliver noticed ribbons attached to notes on some of the branches. As they peered at the cards, Orlando arrived carrying a bucket of his gardening tools. He refused to leave them inside the garden gate overnight, in case they got stolen.

"What are you guys looking at?" Orlando asked.

"'To plant a garden is to be believe in tomorrow,'" Oliver read from one card. "Looks like a lady named Audrey Hepburn gave these plants to us."

Jessie looked over his shoulder, then rolled her eyes. "Audrey Hepburn is the one who *said* it. She's an actress who died a long time ago!"

"How would I know that?" Oliver retorted.

Jessie picked another card. "Look at this one," she said, and read it out loud. "'If you have a garden and a library, you have everything you need.'"

"Audrey Hepburn said that too?" Hyacinth asked.

Orlando chimed in before Jessie could respond. "Marcus Tullius Cicero."

"Yeah," Jessie said, reading the card. "How'd you know that?"

Orlando shrugged.

Hyacinth looked at a card attached to a rose plant, rubbed some dirt from it, and read it out loud.

"It's from *The Secret Garden*!" Hyacinth exclaimed.

"Ooh, there's another one!" Laney said, running to the little tree. "Read it!"

Oliver read the card. "'Every time I doze off, I dream of gardens.' It's from a book called *The Gardener*."

If you look the right way, you can see that the whole world is a garden. ~The Secret Garden

"It looks like these are all from the same person," Jessie observed. "Same handwriting."

"Do you think this mystery-plant-giver person knows this garden might be bulldozed soon?" Oliver said.

Jessie stood up tall. "It only strengthens our case. The more beautiful the garden, the likelier that it gets to stay, right?"

"Where would we even put them?" Oliver said. "There's no space."

"That's no problem," Jessie said. "Orlando and I can install the jug planters on the fence; then we can move the plants from the northeast quadrant into the planters. That will make space to plant the rosebushes and lavender."

Oliver sighed. "Fine, let's put them in." He tried to pick up one of the rosebushes, with little success. He looked over at Orlando, who leaned down and lifted one of the other rosebushes with ease.

Hyacinth raised her hands like a crossing guard in the middle of a busy intersection. "Wait! I want the cards." Orlando set the roses down, and together he and Oliver helped Hyacinth carefully remove the cards. She stored them safely in her knitting pouch.

A blur of movement and the screech of bike tires announced Herman's arrival. He grabbed his big bag of yarn and supplies off the handlebars. "What's with all the plants?" he asked.

After Hyacinth showed off the gorgeous plants and Herman demonstrated sufficient enthusiasm for the new additions, Herman helped lug the pots inside while Orlando and Jessie got to work installing the painted jugs along the fence.

Jessie noticed that Laney kept staring at the area where she had planted Luciana's seeds. She considered telling Laney that she had done some research the night before and found out that seeds—even stored in the best of conditions—could survive for only two to four years. If Luciana had buried that box when she was about four, the seeds would be at least eighteen years old. Laney looked so hopeful about the seeds, however, that Jessie decided she didn't want to be the one to spoil her sister's day.

Hyacinth and Herman spent the rest of the afternoon knitting up a storm. They had only a few more days before the Garden Extravaganza.

During a water break, Hyacinth pulled out the cards with quotes and admired them. "I love these cards," Hyacinth said to Herman. "Whoever wrote them has such beautiful handwriting." The writing was swirly and fancy, as if it had been penned a hundred years ago, when people used feathers dipped into inkwells.

Herman didn't respond; he was knitting a design for the fence so rapidly that his hands, the needles, and the yarn were all a blur.

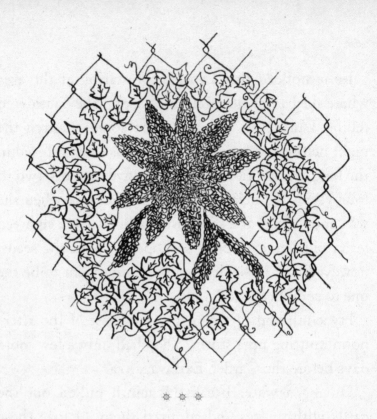

* * *

After lunch and some more weeding, Laney sat next to the circle of bricks and stared at the bare patch of earth inside. It had been ten days since she had sprinkled Luciana's seeds onto the dirt, but there were no signs of life.

"Maybe you're not watering enough," Oliver said to her when she expressed her concern.

"Or you're watering too much," Orlando told her.

"The problem is we don't know what kinds of seeds they are. Maybe they need more light. Or less light."

Laney sighed and stared at the dirt. Why weren't they growing? Meanwhile, her siblings seemed utterly unconcerned. They were pulling weeds, plucking dead leaves and flowers, and building tomato cages from pieces of PVC pipe they had found in Mr. Smiley's basement.

The garden was coming alive, and Laney had to keep herself from poking at Luciana's seeds, urging them to grow.

❂　❂　❂

That night before dinner, Hyacinth plugged in the laminating machine Mr. Beiderman had bought her for her birthday and carefully laid the garden notes between sheets of laminating plastic. When the machine was warmed up, she ran the sheets through. After the laminated sheet came out, she cut off the extra plastic, punched a hole in the corners, and threaded her favorite mauve ribbon through them.

When she went downstairs, everyone was gathered

at the table, about to start dinner. Just as they picked up their utensils to dig in, Mama's phone rang.

"Miss Josie?" Mama said into the phone. Then there was silence, and a big grin spread across her face. She looked at the kids, then said to Miss Josie, "Let me put you on speaker." She clicked the phone button and held it out to Papa and the kids.

Mr. Jeet's rich baritone filled the room. "Love—you," he said.

The kids looked at one another in stunned silence before yelling, "We love you too!"

"Miss—you," he said.

Miss Josie's voice came through the speaker. "He's perked up since your visit. Thank you, sweethearts," she said.

"You can thank us by coming home soon!" Jessie said. Mama brought the phone back to her ear and said a few more words to Miss Josie before putting the phone down.

Mama looked out at her kids, their faces happy and relieved. "The doctors are working on a treatment plan that gets him home by Friday. His occupational therapist said he's been doing great this week with independent walking and going up and down stairs."

"Yay!" cheered Laney.

"He'll be home in time for—" Hyacinth started.

"—Isa's return!" Jessie finished, casting Hyacinth a warning eyebrow raise.

Oliver paused. "Did he really look okay at the hospital?"

"He looked great!" Laney said. "He petted Paganini and everything."

"You should have come, Oliver," Jessie said.

Oliver thought about that day two weeks ago when Mr. Jeet fell down, and he blinked the burn of tears away. "I didn't want to see him all sick."

Mama stood up and wrapped Oliver in a big hug. "We should have a big welcome-home party for him. I'll bake."

Oliver squinted at her. "No green cookies, right?"

Mama paused. "Have I really been that bad?"

The kids nodded.

"Well, let me make it up to you, then. What do you want for dinner?"

"Fried chicken," Jessie said.

"Double-chocolate pecan cookies," Oliver said.

"Macaroni and cheese," Hyacinth said.

"Bread," Laney said. "Lots of bread."

Mama smiled. "Done."

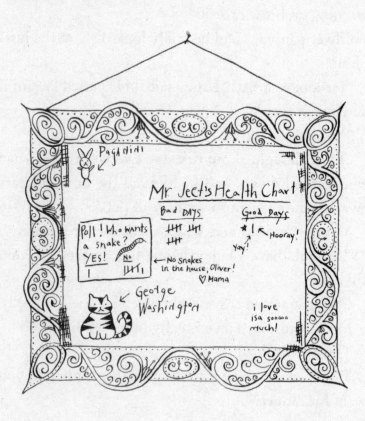

THURSDAY, JULY 12

Days Mr. Jeet in Hospital: 17

Days Until Garden
Extravaganza: 2

Twenty-Six

On Thursday morning, the Vanderbeekers headed to the garden with buoyant hearts. Mr. Jeet and Miss Josie were coming home, the garden was thriving, and there had been no word from the contractors for eleven days. About halfway down the street, they could see Herman Huxley's familiar slouch next to the garden gates.

"He looks like he's doing something to the fence," Hyacinth commented, squinting down the street.

"He really shouldn't draw attention to the garden like that," Oliver said. "People will get suspicious."

Herman turned his head and spotted them, and when they got close, he quickly threw what looked like a knitted blanket onto the fence and stood in front of it.

Hyacinth stared at him. "What are you doing?"

Jessie spoke. "That blanket draws attention to our garden, don't you think?" She reached over to pull it down, and Herman tried to block her. Jessie had an extra six inches on him and was able to reach over his head; she easily grabbed the edge of the blanket, pulling it down with one yank. Underneath it was a sign.

"I'm sorry," Herman said miserably. "It was here when I got here. I didn't want you to see it."

Oliver ran to the gate and pushed away the ivy. The new bike lock was gone, replaced with an imposing heavy-duty lock that looked impossible to open without a jackhammer. On the ground were metal shards of the bike lock, as if someone had used power tools to break it.

"I cannot *believe* this," Jessie fumed. She jammed a stick she found on the sidewalk through the fence, hoping to peek inside to see if there was any damage, but the ivy was too thick. She shook the gate in frustration.

Oliver tried to climb the fence, but his feet kept slipping because of the twisting vines that covered it.

"It wouldn't matter even if you could climb it," Jessie said, pointing to the top of the fence, where someone had spiraled fresh barbed wire.

"Our garden is going to be bulldozed, and we'll never see whether Luciana's seeds have grown, and Mr. Jeet and Miss Josie won't ever sit under the Silver Queen and Tilia of the Eternal Spring and hear the birds chirping," Hyacinth said.

"I can't believe we're so close, and now . . ." Jessie trailed off.

". . . it's gone," Hyacinth finished.

"Too bad Mr. Beiderman can't get his friend to

protect it," Laney said, leaning against the fence and trying to bury herself in the ivy. "He has a friend who saves buildings."

There was a pause before Jessie said, "How do you know that?"

"I heard him on the phone," Laney said.

Jessie looked at the church. "This church is one of the oldest in the city. I remember Miss Josie telling me it used to be a safe stop for people traveling along the Underground Railroad."

"So let's talk to this Mr. Beiderman guy," Herman said. "What are we waiting for?"

The Vanderbeekers hesitated. "We haven't told any adults about the garden yet. And Mr. Beiderman has a . . . history here. Back when this was a preschool, we think his daughter, Luciana, went here," Jessie said.

Herman threw his hands up. "Wouldn't that make him want to save it more?"

Hyacinth looked at her siblings, then back at Herman. "Luciana is dead, and Mr. Beiderman hasn't left his home in over six years."

Herman opened his mouth, then closed his mouth, then opened it again. "He's your only hope right now," he said. "Triple J still hasn't come back, right? Has he called you?"

Jessie shook her head. "I don't know why he suddenly disappeared, and I don't understand how the land could have been sold without his permission. I've left a dozen messages on his phone."

Oliver turned on his heel and started walking back home. "I think Herman is right. Mr. Beiderman *is* our only hope."

❋ ❋ ❋

"You knock," Oliver told Herman. "It was your idea."

"No way," Herman called from behind the Vanderbeeker family. "I've never even met this dude."

"Hyacinth, you do it. You're his favorite," Jessie suggested.

She shook her head. "Laney, you love knocking on doors."

Laney bit her lip. "I don't want to bring up Luciana. It makes him too sad."

From inside the apartment, Mr. Beiderman yelled, "What's the racket? Come in, already!"

Jessie looked at her siblings and Herman, then opened the door. Everyone filed inside.

"Who are you?" Mr. Beiderman demanded when he saw Herman, who kept one foot outside the door.

"This is Herman Huxley," Oliver said. "My friend from school."

Mr. Beiderman sized Herman up and deemed him worthy. "Come in. I'm not going to bite," he grumbled. Herman shrugged, then stepped into the apartment and closed the door behind him. Princess Cutie leaped off the couch and landed at his feet, then batted his shoelaces with her paws. Herman leaned down to stroke her forehead.

"To what do I owe this pleasure?" Mr. Beiderman asked.

Jessie nudged Oliver, Oliver nudged Hyacinth, and Hyacinth tried to nudge Laney, but she had crawled under Mr. Beiderman's kitchen table and was out of reach.

Finally, Hyacinth spoke. "We started a project. Down the street by the church."

Mr. Beiderman raised his eyebrows. "You think I

don't know where you've been disappearing to all these weeks?"

Hyacinth, remembering the garden gloves, stared at him. "How *did* you know?"

"I looked out my window," he said.

The Vanderbeekers rushed to the window overlooking 141st Street and looked out, and sure enough, there was a clear view down the street from the third floor.

Jessie turned around. "Well, okay, then. We wanted to do something special for Mr. Jeet and Miss Josie—"

Mr. Beiderman waved her words away. "Yes, I know. I've seen you bring flowers and gardening supplies in there."

"Did it bother you?" Hyacinth asked.

"Why would it?"

"Because Luciana went to that school," Oliver said.

"How did you— Oh, never mind," Mr. Beiderman said. "It didn't bother me. I think it's nice."

"Boy, am I glad you said that," Oliver breathed, "because we need to ask you a huge favor. That person you know, the one who saves the buildings . . . can you call them? Because a sign appeared in front of our garden that says the land is sold. We overheard people talking about putting a condo there. Triple J is nowhere to be found, and the only thing we can think to do is ask your friend for help."

Mr. Beiderman's eyebrows rose. "They're selling the church?"

"No, just the land next to it," Jessie clarified.

Mr. Beiderman shook his head. "I don't know if my friend can help if it's already sold. It's land, not a building . . ."

"But it's part of the building's history," Oliver said. "Right?"

"Miss Josie said it was a stop on the Underground Railroad," Hyacinth added.

"It's of historical importance," Jessie said. "A treasure."

"And your daughter buried stuff there!" Laney finished, pulling Luciana's box from the front pocket of her backpack and holding it out to Mr. Beiderman.

Everyone stilled. Showing Mr. Beiderman Luciana's box was *not* part of the plan.

"But how did you— That was— She loved that box," Mr. Beiderman stammered. He reached out slowly, as if it were a ghost and would disappear if he touched it. Gently he picked it up and opened the latch, his fingers tracing the writing inside. "I made this for her. She used to store seeds from her mother's garden in here; she said they were magic." He closed the box, and his fingers wrapped around it, as if trying to hold on to all the memories that opening it had conjured.

"So . . . can you help us?" Laney asked.

"You're the garden's last hope," Jessie said.

"Please," Oliver said, picking up Mr. Beiderman's phone and handing it to him. "Please."

Twenty-Seven

I can't believe I'm doing this," Mr. Beiderman said.
He had just hung up with Ms. Lin from New York
City's Landmarks Preservation Commission. She told
him that in order to start the process immediately,
they would have to go downtown to the office.

In person.

There was paperwork to fill out, Ms. Lin had told
him, and signatures, and it all had to be notarized.
This had to be done by the weekend if there was any
hope of stopping a sale that was already in progress.
The office closed at five o'clock sharp, and it was
already past three.

"Put on this purple tie," Laney said, rummaging
through his drawers. "It's my favorite color."

"I haven't worn a tie in six years."

"Believe me, you will look fancy," Hyacinth said. "Franz looks great in purple, too."

"Stand still," Jessie said. "I can't comb your hair when you're jiggling around."

"I don't want my hair combed," Mr. Beiderman said, swatting her hand away. "It's fine."

"You've cut it yourself for nearly a decade," Oliver said, "and it shows. You're going to scare the people."

Mr. Beiderman looped the tie around his neck and did a complicated twisting thing that made it into a neat knot. Hyacinth tried to remember the steps so she could help Franz put on a tie one day. Then he put his arms out to the side and glared at them. "How do I look?"

"You look very handsome," Laney said, jumping from foot to foot.

"No one is going to mistake you for a werewolf," Hyacinth said solemnly.

"Do you have everything you need?" Jessie asked.

"Are you ready?" Oliver asked.

"Of course he's ready," Laney said. She took his hand and they went down two flights, the stairs creaking happily as they descended.

Jessie opened the door of the brownstone, and the street spread out before them. Trees filtered dappled sunlight onto the sidewalks and against the buildings, and a cab honked as it veered around a mail truck.

Mr. Beiderman stood in the doorway and shaded his eyes. He looked up and down the street, and he squeezed Laney's hand.

Then he stepped outside the brownstone for the first time in six years.

* * *

The Vanderbeekers led Mr. Beiderman to the subway, saying goodbye to Herman at Adam Clayton Powell Jr. Boulevard. He needed to get home because he always had a video call with his mom on Thursdays at four thirty.

Hyacinth was worried about Mr. Beiderman. He hadn't left the brownstone in years, and now he had to walk down the street and all the way to the subway, dodging late-afternoon summer-camp groups, mail carriers, kids on scooters, and dogs on leashes. The sun was bright against his skin, and the wind from passing traffic blew his hair straight up in the air. Hyacinth felt as if the honking cars and squealing bus breaks were louder than usual, and she fretted about Mr. Beiderman's sensitive ears.

They descended into the subway station, and Hyacinth watched as Mr. Beiderman fumbled for his wallet and unearthed a faded MetroCard. It had expired years ago, so Jessie swiped him through with her card and dragged him onto the number three train right before the doors closed.

The train, which originated only one stop away, was mostly empty, and they found five seats in a row with no problem. They put Mr. Beiderman in the middle, with Laney and Jessie on one side of him and Hyacinth and Oliver on the other side, the better to keep him from bolting. He kept checking his pockets for his wallet and cell phone and subway directions to the Preservation Commission offices and avoided eye contact with anyone.

"Are you nervous?" Laney asked him.

Mr. Beiderman wiped his brow with a handkerchief and stared at a subway pole. "Of course not."

Laney glanced at his trembling hands gripping his

checkered handkerchief, then changed the subject. "Did you know foxes come from the dog family?"

Mr. Beiderman checked his pockets for the directions again, then said, "I did know foxes come from the dog family." Then he closed his eyes, as if needing to shut out the world.

The Vanderbeekers fell into silence as the train rumbled downtown. Hyacinth leaned against Mr. Beiderman's shoulder and did some finger knitting, Jessie fiddled with her phone, Oliver tapped his feet on the ground and read every one of the subway advertisements, and Laney struck up a conversation with the stranger next to her about how she wished Mama would buy her shoes with heels. Passengers got off, but more people got on, and the train soon filled with all sorts of people, including a group wearing fancy clothes and carrying bunches of balloons with glitter inside them.

As Hyacinth wrapped yarn around her fingers, she wondered if Mr. Beiderman was okay. She had always imagined that his first time outside would be to their backyard, or a few blocks away to Castleman's Bakery.

But instead, they had asked so much of him; not only did he leave the brownstone, but he was now underground and traveling all the way to the bottom of Manhattan. She felt him take in a deep breath, then release it in a shaky exhale. Hyacinth wondered if he would make it all the way downtown.

They were on the subway forever, and Hyacinth overheard Laney ask Oliver *again* how many stops they had left. When Oliver announced that they were only two stops away, Laney cheered at the exact moment the subway groaned to a stop in the middle of the subway tunnel. The lights flickered. Mr. Beiderman opened his eyes and looked around. Other passengers sighed and glanced at their watches.

Oliver looked over at Jessie. "What time is it?" he asked.

She looked at her watch. "Four-oh-eight. Fifty-two minutes before the office closes."

Mr. Beiderman's lips set in a straight line.

"It'll get moving soon," Hyacinth assured him, hoping what she said was true. "This happens all the time."

Then a muffled subway announcement said, "Due

to a police investigation at Chambers Street, all downtown express trains are being delayed. We apologize for the inconvenience."

✵ ✵ ✵

There were stages to how subway passengers reacted to delays, Jessie thought. Within the first fifteen minutes, people would talk to one another about what they were going to be late for. The guy across from them, who was wearing a crisp business suit, was telling the woman next to him that he had a meeting at four thirty. The woman was wearing her baby in a sling and trying to keep it from waking up by rocking it back and forth to mimic subway movements.

Laney, who had been chatting with the woman next to her the whole way down, started telling her all about the garden, and how it was going to be bulldozed over if they didn't get to the building-saving people who worked for the government. The woman asked lots of questions, and Oliver soon joined in on the conversation while people around them shamelessly eavesdropped.

Jessie could hear the story spreading around the subway car in bits and pieces.

"Did you hear about those kids?" a guy holding a skateboard was saying to his friend. "They're trying to save a garden on their block from being made into a condo. They need to get to a government office by five."

Another subway announcement came on, saying that the police investigation was ongoing and all express trains were delayed and they apologized for the inconvenience. Jessie looked at her watch again. Half an hour had gone by. By then, the whole subway car was looking at the kids sympathetically, which was made worse by the fact that Oliver had told both Laney and Hyacinth that they weren't going to make it in time. Now both sisters were crying.

At five o'clock, when all hope was gone, the subway riders started murmuring sympathies to the kids. Jessie, however, was more worried about Mr. Beiderman. He hadn't spoken since right after entering the subway, and the tremors in his hands had become more pronounced. She wondered what they would do if he needed medical help. Just when she considered asking whether anyone on the train was a doctor, the subway lurched, and a few minutes later it rolled into the station. The doors opened and the Vanderbeekers filed out onto the platform, Mr. Beiderman's hand in Hyacinth's.

It was 5:37 p.m.

Jessie wordlessly led her siblings and Mr. Beiderman up over the overpass and back downstairs to the track for the uptown trains. No need to even try to go to the government office; it was too late for that.

Jessie had learned a lot about her family in the past few years, and she knew they would bounce back . . . eventually. Maybe the garden next to the church, the way they'd dreamed it up, wasn't meant to be. Maybe they would find another spot, another neglected lot, that needed the Vanderbeeker treatment.

Surely this wasn't the end of the story.

✦ ✦ ✦

That night, the Vanderbeekers went up to the roof. It was a dark, cloudy night, and Harlem spread out around them in a matrix of buildings and streets. They leaned against the ledge and looked out at the city.

"I hope Mr. Beiderman is okay," Hyacinth said. By the time the subway had brought them back up to Harlem, Mr. Beiderman was so silent and exhausted that once they reached the brownstone, it took him five minutes to climb up to the third floor, his hand gripping the banister the whole way up. He shut the door behind him without saying goodbye.

"He's never going to leave the brownstone again," Oliver said. "We've ruined him forever."

"We didn't *ruin* him," Jessie said. "But we may have . . . rushed him."

"He needs some alone time," Laney said, repeating a phrase her parents used frequently.

"I wonder how our plants are doing," Hyacinth said. She turned her head to see if she could glimpse inside their garden, but buildings obscured her view. "The Silver Queen and Tilia of the Eternal Spring miss us."

"Maybe the builders will let us in before they begin construction," Jessie said. "Maybe we can relocate the plants."

"Yeah, maybe," Oliver said. "But where?"

"Our backyard, for now," Jessie suggested.

"I guess." Oliver thought about their backyard,

which was about one-tenth the size of the garden and already full of plants. "That garden felt like the perfect place for Miss Josie and Mr. Jeet."

"It felt like the perfect place for us too," Jessie said.

"Can we take the Silver Queen with us?" Laney asked.

"No," Oliver answered. "She's too big. They'll chop her down."

Hyacinth's heart gave a painful thump as she considered the Silver Queen, a tree that had watched over 141st Street for decades, being cut down.

She took a deep breath, and a light rain began to pitter-patter against the tiled roof floor. "I wish Mr. Jeet and Miss Josie could sit under the Silver Queen just once before we say goodbye to the garden."

And the rest of the Vanderbeekers silently agreed, dwelling on that image and holding it close to their hearts as they descended the fire-escape stairs and slipped back inside the brownstone.

FRIDAY, JULY 13

Days Until Garden
Extravaganza: 1

Twenty-Eight

ISA: Is Mr. B coming to my concert?

JESSIE: No.

ISA: Are you sure??? Ask him one more time. We're playing Luciana's favorite piece.

JESSIE: Okay. But don't be sad when he doesn't show up.

ISA: Did you pack barf buckets for Laney?

JESSIE: Yes.

ISA: And everyone has backup clothes?

JESSIE: Yes.

ISA: Because remember the last time—

JESSIE: I REMEMBER. I'M TRYING TO FORGET.

ISA: Okay! See you soon. I'm looking forward to sleeping in my bed again. The bed here is so lumpy.

❖ ❖ ❖

Jessie glanced at Isa's bed, which still had that chocolate stain from a few weeks ago. Isa's usually smooth covers had permanent wrinkles from all the times Laney and Hyacinth had burrowed themselves into her bed because they missed her. Jessie's messy habits had slowly crept over to Isa's side, so science books, food wrappers, and dirty clothes were now evenly scattered throughout the room. Hopefully Isa would be so happy to be home that she wouldn't get too mad.

There was a good, soaking rain when Miss Josie and Mr. Jeet finally came home that morning. Mama and Papa had warned the kids not to overwhelm them when they arrived, but when Miss Josie and Mr. Jeet came out of the cab, both Mama and Papa ignored their own advice and rushed over with umbrellas and started fussing and asking a million questions. Then Mama started crying, her tears dripping on Mr. Jeet's shirt, so Jessie nudged her out of the way and helped Mr. Jeet herself. Oliver took Miss Josie's hand, and Hyacinth and Laney lugged their bags up the stairs of the brownstone. They helped them into the apartment, which had been cleaned multiple times and stocked with enough healthy food to last for weeks.

After settling Mr. Jeet and Miss Josie in, the Vanderbeekers went back downstairs to get ready to leave for Isa's concert. It would take four hours to get to Ferris Lake, and while the Vanderbeekers were not looking forward to the long drive, they couldn't wait to see their Isa. Finally, everyone who belonged in the brownstone would be back again.

Jessie finished packing her bag with a biography of the botanist Maria Merian (it had caught her eye at the library), her notebook, peppermint drops for Laney for when she started getting carsick, and headphones to block out the inevitable family sing-along.

Jessie ran downstairs, grabbed her raincoat and an umbrella, and joined everyone else on the sidewalk in front of the brownstone. They waited at the curb while Papa retrieved the car they were using for the trip. Mama was interrogating Oliver about his outfit.

"Why aren't you wearing slacks and that nice button-down shirt Grandma gave you?" she asked him.

Jessie watched her brother squirm. "Um, I sort of sold them."

"Sold your nice clothes!" Mama exclaimed. "Why would you do that?"

Jessie didn't want to hang around to hear the rest of that conversation. "I'm going to run up and double-check one last time whether Mr. Beiderman wants to join us," she said to them. She closed her umbrella, and ran up the three flights—forty-four steps—and banged on the door.

There was no answer. She knocked again. "Mr. Beiderman! We're leaving for Isa's concert. Can you come?"

After another minute, she ran back down the stairs and put her umbrella up.

"No answer," Jessie announced, not that she was surprised.

Hyacinth went up next, but she was back a minute later. "He's not responding," she said. "I think he wants to be alone."

Laney wanted to give it one last try. She dug around in her bag and pulled out her precious green M&M's jar. "I'll go!" she said cheerfully, being careful not to shake the jar and crack the perfect M&M's.

Jessie, Oliver, and Hyacinth watched. Maybe Mr. Beiderman wouldn't be able to resist Laney.

Mama spoke while squinting at a traffic map on her phone. "Hurry up!" she said to her phone, and the kids assumed she was talking to Papa, even though he was nowhere in sight.

Laney hopped up the steps on one foot in her clunky pink rain boots, pretending to be a flamingo, while her siblings hollered, "Hold the handrails!" and "Be careful!" and "Walk up normally, for heaven's sake!" Laney didn't appear to understand anything they were saying, because she continued hopping all the way to the top and pushed through the brownstone door. She was gone longer than everyone else.

Laney came back outside at the exact moment that Miss Josie opened her second-floor window and called, "Don't forget to record the performance for us!" and Papa rolled up to the curb and beeped the horn. The vehicle Papa was driving was not the nice, clean-smelling rental car they had all been crossing their fingers for. The windshield wipers were squeaking, working overtime to wipe the rain off the front windshield. At the sight of the van, Oliver was too busy making gagging noises; Jessie was too busy nudging Mama and saying, "We're not *really* going in that, are we?"; and Hyacinth was too busy waving to Franz through the apartment window to notice that Laney had returned without her green M&M's jar.

❖ ❖ ❖

The Vanderbeekers did not own a car, so when they needed to get out of the city, they either rented a car or borrowed a car from a neighbor. When Papa rolled up in Mr. Smiley's van, everyone groaned.

"Maybe it won't smell," Mama said optimistically.

Papa stepped out of the car and gasped as if he had been holding his breath. After he had pulled fresh air into his lungs, he looked at his horrified family and said, "Ready?"

"I am *not* going in there," Oliver reported. He jabbed a thumb behind his shoulder at Laney. "Because you-know-who has the you-know-what problem."

Mama sighed and started toward the van. "Come on, troops. We might not hit traffic if we leave right now. Isa is waiting for us."

"It smells better than it did last time," Papa said encouragingly.

Given that Mr. Smiley was an avid fisherman, Jessie doubted it. She glared at her father. "Don't even talk to us," she said.

"It was a last resort," he explained. "The amount of money the rental companies charge for a car on a Friday is extortion."

"You should have paid it," Oliver mumbled as he pinched his nose and climbed inside, cracking all the windows open before he buckled himself in. They made Laney sit next to a window that could roll down all the way, and off they went. Everyone kept their raincoats on, because it was going to be a long, wet ride.

Jessie thought about the garden as Papa revved up the van. She wondered how the plants were doing and whether they were happy to get some rain. It was funny how attached Jessie had gotten to the garden and plants in a few short weeks. She thought about the birds and wondered whether they missed hearing the kids talking and singing. She even wanted to see the pesky squirrel that liked to dig up parts of the garden in his search for nuts.

Jessie had never thought botany was her thing, but after only two weeks in the garden, the miracle of seeds and soil thrilled her. She would miss entering that peaceful haven, with the sunlight filtering through the leaves, the way the light would cast a dappled glow on everyone's faces. She would miss the joy of watching a plant grow a little bigger each day, and studying flower buds that would one day turn into a tomato or a zucchini. She would miss the way the garden rustled with happiness every time they stepped inside.

The loss felt so heavy on Jessie's heart that when the van chugged down the street, she had to turn her head away from the church and its gated garden so she wouldn't catch a glimpse of the place they would never enter again.

* * *

Their two biggest worries—Friday traffic and Laney getting carsick—turned out not to be problems. Laney ate precisely twenty-three peppermint drops and threw up just twice. The only bad thing about the peppermint-candy consumption was that she was even bouncier than usual after all that sugar.

It had rained the entire ride up, and given the choice between fishy van smell and fresh air, they unanimously chose fresh air and kept all the windows cracked. They arrived at Isa's concert a whole ten minutes early, everyone damp from the rain. While Mama and Papa dried the van's interior with stacks of paper towels, Oliver set up Papa's phone so he could livestream the event for Mr. Jeet and Miss Josie.

They got seated in the concert hall just as Isa walked onto the stage in her long black dress; Hyacinth almost didn't recognize her. Instead of the usual slick ponytail, Isa's hair was in a braid that wrapped all the way around her head like a crown. She took her place as first chair of the second-violin section, and she looked so confident and regal that none of the Vanderbeekers doubted that being up onstage, playing the violin, was what Isa was meant to do.

The concert was beautiful (even though Oliver *did* think it was unnecessarily long), and the Vanderbeekers were the first of the audience to leap out of their seats to give a standing ovation. They clapped so much, their hands hurt. When the orchestra finally left the stage, the Vanderbeekers exited the concert hall and milled around the fancy lobby, where a sparkly chandelier hung from the ceiling and a red carpet covered the floor. Laney was weaving in and out of the banister of the grand staircase when Isa came out in her black dress with her instrument and luggage. After the Vanderbeekers descended on her and gave her enough hugs and kisses to make up for her having been gone for three whole weeks, Oliver eyed her dress.

"You'll want to change," he advised her.

"Why?" she asked. "I don't mind wearing this. My shorts are buried way at the bottom of the luggage, and I don't want to pull them out."

"Trust us," Jessie said. "You don't want your nicest dress to smell like fish."

"But why would it—" Isa began; then, "Oh no."

"Oh yes," Oliver replied.

"Welcome home!" Hyacinth announced as she led the way to the parking lot and the fish van.

Saturday, July 14

Days Until Garden
Extravaganza: 0

Twenty-Nine

The next morning brought bright blue skies and fresh air after the previous day's rain, and every one of the brownstone's windows was open, letting in a cool breeze. On the first floor, the brownstone creaked with happiness in the twins' room as Isa woke up and ran her fingers against the rough brick wall next to her bed. Jessie was still asleep, tangled in her covers, her mouth open and her arm flopped over her face.

In the next bedroom, Oliver mumbled in his sleep. He was dreaming about running down the basketball court, about to make the perfect lay-up. Then he noticed Mr. B jogging next to him, wearing a black-and-white referee shirt and blowing a whistle. Oliver tried to focus on the basket ahead of him, but Mr. B was so persistent! Oliver jerked himself awake to find George Washington nuzzling his head and Laney playing her kazoo right next to his ear. He squeezed his eyes shut, and Laney put her kazoo down on his stomach and pried one of his eyes open.

"I love you, Oli," she said.

In the next bedroom, Hyacinth lay in a dreamless slumber in her bunk bed. Franz, however, sat as straight as a member of the Queen's Guard, ready to spring into action the second she woke up.

In the last bedroom on the floor, Mama and Papa were so sound asleep that it would take all five Vanderbeeker kids jumping on their bed half an hour later to wake them up.

Upstairs on the second floor, Mr. Jeet sat on his bed while Miss Josie worked on his bow tie. Once she was done, she gave him a kiss on his forehead. Mr. Jeet put his hand in hers, braced his other hand against the end table, and took a deep breath. Then he stood up, and slowly, slowly they walked toward the kitchen for their morning cup of coffee.

And up on the top floor, Mr. Beiderman put food into Princess Cutie's food bowl while she rubbed her head against his freshly ironed suit pants. He looked out the window, one hand against the window frame. A breeze brushed his face. Then he dabbed at his forehead with the handkerchief he kept in his pocket, closed his eyes, and prepared himself for the day to come.

* * *

Jessie woke to the sound of Isa plucking her violin strings. She had really missed waking up to that. Above her, she could hear Miss Josie's gentle footsteps and the joyful creak of floorboards. Today hadn't ended up the way she had imagined it would, with a giant welcome-home party in their secret garden, but this was enough.

Isa, noticing that Jessie was awake, smiled in her direction.

"I wish I could show you the garden," Jessie said. "You would have loved it."

"We could walk over there now," Isa suggested.

"We can't get inside anymore."

"I'd like to see the outside anyway. Then we could walk to Castleman's and get breakfast."

Jessie raised her eyebrows. "You want to see Benjamin!"

Isa flushed. "I want a cheese croissant, okay? You coming or not?"

It turned out everyone was hungry for Castleman's, including Mama and Papa. So they all changed out of their pajamas and headed out the door and across 141st Street.

Hyacinth noticed the commotion first. She pointed it out to Oliver, who pointed it out to Jessie and Isa, who pointed it out to Laney. A small crowd was gathered in front of the garden. As they drew closer, they recognized Mr. Huxley and Herman. Triple J stood next to him with a bulging suitcase.

"Triple J!" Laney cried, running toward him.

"Laney Bean!" Triple J called, then caught her and swung her around.

"Where have you been?" Jessie cried.

"We've left so many messages!" Oliver exclaimed.

"Did you know *he's* selling your land?" Hyacinth added, pointing a finger at Mr. Huxley.

Triple J glanced from Vanderbeeker to Vanderbeeker,

answering their questions. "I've been in South Carolina, helping my brother. He fell down the stairs and broke his leg. I'm afraid my phone fell out of my pocket at the airport and shattered, and when I tried to get a new one, the phone company told me I needed to give them my password, which I didn't even know I had created. So I had to get a new phone number and I lost all my messages. And," he said to Hyacinth, "I'm finding out about this land thing right now."

"You asked me to find ways for us to repair the roof and replace the boiler," Mr. Huxley said, annoyed. "This deal came along, and it was too good to let pass. I tried to call, but you were unreachable. I made the best decision I could, given the circumstances. I don't need to tell you how critical it is for us to act swiftly before this church crumbles to the ground."

"You should have waited until I returned," Triple J said, shaking his head. "I was only away for a couple of weeks."

Mr. Huxley sniffed. "You know how these land developers are. Once you get an attractive offer, you've got to move on it."

The Vanderbeekers looked at him with distrust.

"If it's such hot property," Oliver pointed out, "you would have gotten more money if you'd waited longer."

"It's called the law of demand," Jessie said. "It's a basic economic theory."

"Wait," Papa said, confused. "What's going on here?"

Mr. Huxley ignored Papa. "As treasurer of the church, I have the authority to sign off on *all* the necessary paperwork. It's a done deal."

Herman, who had been mostly quiet during the whole interchange, shook his head. "Dad, there must be another way."

"This doesn't concern you," Mr. Huxley said sharply, and the Vanderbeeker kids instinctively took a step closer to Herman.

"Have you looked inside the gates, Mr. Huxley?" Jessie said. "Have you seen what's there? What you're destroying?"

"Wait," Mama said, trying to follow along. "What's inside where?"

"Tilia of the Eternal Spring is in there! And the

Silver Queen—she's over one hundred years old!" Hyacinth said. "They're scared all by themselves."

"We could have enough vegetables to feed the whole block," Oliver added.

"We worked so hard on it," Herman said. "At least take one look."

"I didn't even know you were using it," Triple J said. "How'd you get inside?"

"I want to see it," Papa said, looking around. "Whatever 'it' is."

"No one needs to see anything," Mr. Huxley snapped. "The land is sold. Nothing can be done, unless the church wants to be sued for breach of contract."

The kids sucked in a breath. Could the church really be sued? Before another word was spoken, a swift wind swept down 141st Street, rustling the ivy on the garden fence so fiercely that it sounded like a stadium cheer swelling to a roar.

"I find it peculiar," came a voice from behind them, "that you sold this land without properly researching its historical significance."

Everyone froze, then slowly turned around. There,

standing tall, with the sun behind him and the leaves rustling all around him, stood Mr. Beiderman.

Mr. Huxley's voice lowered. "I don't know who you are—"

"I am Arthur Beiderman," he said, his voice clear and strong. "I was a member of this church for nearly two decades, until six years ago. My wife and I said our vows at the altar in front of friends and family. When our daughter, Luciana, came along, she learned how to climb stairs by practicing on those steps." He pointed to the wide steps leading to the church door. "She made her first friends at the church preschool, and played on that land you want to build on top of."

Mr. Huxley sniffed. "You certainly don't expect the church to renege on a sale just because your daughter—"

"She also played on the same land where Adam Clayton Powell, Jr., once stood," Mr. Beiderman continued. "The same Adam Clayton Powell, Jr., who preached the good news as a pastor and campaigned here for the House of Representatives in 1944."

"A street is named after him!" Laney said excitedly.

"And finally, according to many lifelong Harlem residents and a dozen highly esteemed researchers, this is the same land where a safe house for the Underground Railroad stood, sheltering people escaping slavery as they fled north."

"How—how can you even prove that?" Mr. Huxley stammered.

"I have the proof right here," Mr. Beiderman said, pulling books and file folders bulging with papers out of a ragged briefcase. "I had help from the local library, and the librarians assured me they have much more material if needed. My friend Ms. Lin of the Landmarks Preservation Commission is so eager to maintain important pieces of Harlem that she kindly expedited the paperwork, plus a judge was notified of the situation and placed a cease-and-desist order on the land sale. I'm sure you'll be notified soon. She's thrilled that a garden has been planted on the land, and she plans to put up a plaque commemorating the space once the paperwork is official."

Mr. Beiderman paused to take a breath, then to look at the Vanderbeeker kids, whose jaws had dropped in amazement. "And of course, I had help from my friends, who showed me how to live again, for which I am endlessly thankful."

He leaned down and pulled one last item from his bag: a jar of green M&M's, which he handed back to Laney. "Thank you for all this luck. I only needed a couple."

Thirty

Mr. Huxley had stormed off, phone to ear, dragging Herman behind him. The Vanderbeekers watched them disappear around the corner, and then they turned back to Mr. Beiderman.

"I can't believe you're here!" Laney said, wrapping her arms around his waist.

"You're our hero!" Jessie exclaimed.

"Are you okay?" Hyacinth asked him. "You know, because . . ."

Mr. Beiderman cleared his throat. "I figured if I could survive getting stuck on the subway for hours, I could survive going out again yesterday."

"Can someone please tell us what's going on?" Mama

demanded at the same time Papa said, "That's it, everyone is grounded until I know what's happening."

Mr. Beiderman raised his hand in surrender. "Don't look at me. I haven't even seen the inside."

"Inside *what*?" Papa gritted out.

"Inside there," Laney informed her parents, pointing to the fence. "Oliver picked the lock."

"He *what*?" Mama and Papa said.

Jessie spoke up. "I wish we could show you what it looks like, but I doubt Mr. Huxley is going to come back and open it for us. He changed the lock, and now we can't get in."

Mama dialed a number and put her phone to her ear. "Arthur? If you're around, can you come quick? Also, can you bring your industrial bolt cutter?"

☙ ☙ ☙

Triple J and Mr. Beiderman stood guard by the fence, just in case Mr. Huxley or the land developers dared to return, while the Vanderbeekers ran home to fetch Mr. Jeet and Miss Josie. It took time for them to walk to the garden, Mr. Jeet carefully navigating his walker, but they arrived just as Uncle Arthur and Auntie Harrigan pulled up in their black pickup truck. Since Uncle Arthur worked in construction, the Vanderbeekers depended on him for all their specialty-tool needs.

"Did someone call for an industrial bolt cutter?" he hollered from the driver's-side window.

The Vanderbeekers cheered, and Mr. Jeet and Miss Josie smiled politely, despite wondering why they were all standing on the sidewalk for no apparent reason.

Uncle Arthur squeezed into a No Parking zone and jumped out of the truck with the bolt cutter, followed by Auntie Harrigan, who was wearing a red summer dress, her hair dyed the colors of a mermaid's tail.

The kids showed him where the lock hung on the gate, and without asking a single question, he began the countdown.

"Three!" he yelled.

"Two!" yelled the kids.

"Wait!" came a voice.

Everyone swiveled to find Herman, Orlando, Benjamin, and Angie running down the street.

"Benny!" Isa yelled.

When Benjamin reached her, they greeted each other with a happy, awkward hug. Herman, winded, rested his hands on his knees to catch his breath.

"I'm—so—sorry—about Dad," he rasped.

Laney tackled him in a hug, and Hyacinth said, "We're glad you're here," and when Oliver slugged him on the shoulder and said, "You're not so bad," Herman lit up like a dozen fireflies.

"Should we try again?" Uncle Arthur asked.

"Yes!" everyone yelled.

And with a swift yank on the bolt cutters, the lock fell from the chain and everyone pushed the gate open and stepped inside.

* * *

Miss Josie gasped and Mr. Jeet's jaw dropped as they took in the sight. The Vanderbeekers led them in slowly, allowing them to absorb the scene.

"You did it," Miss Josie whispered. "I can't believe it."

Then Laney shrieked and pointed toward the

middle of the garden, where a spray of flowers exploded from inside the brick circle.

"Her flowers grew!" Laney cried, running to them.

Mr. Beiderman followed her, his eyes wide in shock. When he got there, he reached out to touch a spray of black-eyed Susans, bright yellow flowers with fuzzy brown centers.

The rest of the crowd arrived and gathered around the display.

"Those were the seeds in Luciana's box," Laney told them. "We planted them and Jessie said they were too old to bloom but she was wrong because—see!"

And no one could dispute that, because right there was the proof that seeds could grow even in the mostly unlikely of circumstances.

"We need to study those seeds," Jessie told Orlando.

"Maybe it was the rain?" Orlando offered. They both looked up at the sky, then leaned in for a closer inspection of the flowers.

Mama and Papa walked around in utter confusion, saying things like "You planted all this?" and "How is this possible?" Jessie and Orlando tinkered with something mysterious near the lavender plants. Mr. Jeet, Miss Josie, and Mr. Beiderman oohed and aahed over the recycled planters that hung from the western fence by the church, the knitted bench, Tilia of the Eternal Spring and the Silver Queen, the yarn bombing, and the fruit and vegetable gardens.

Finally, Jessie gave Oliver the thumbs-up signal.

"Mr. Jeet, Miss Josie, Mr. Beiderman!" Oliver called from the northeast corner of the garden. "We have something to show you."

Mr. Jeet and Miss Josie made their way over at once, but Mr. Beiderman shook his head, as if he couldn't take in one thing more. Laney grabbed his hand and dragged him to where the lavender grew. A recycled plastic planter painted to look like a groundhog sat at the entrance.

"Welcome to our lavender maze!" Hyacinth said with a sweeping gesture, as if she were greeting royalty.

Mr. Beiderman, Miss Josie, and Mr. Jeet stepped onto the path, and the sound of music filled the air. It was a waltz called "Roses from the South" by Johann

Strauss II, recorded during Isa's orchestra concert and downloaded so it played on the wireless speakers Jessie and Orlando had just set up.

"You told Hyacinth that Luciana said music helped plants grow," Oliver explained. "And we know her favorite plants were lavender."

"But—" Mr. Beiderman spluttered.

"We recorded Isa's concert—" Jessie started.

"—and we set up these old speakers we found in the electronics recycling bin in Mr. Smiley's building," Orlando said.

"Then we installed a motion sensor in Laney's goat planter—"

"It's a groundhog!" Laney corrected her sister.

"—and now it will always play Luciana's favorite music when someone walks through the lavender maze," Jessie finished.

Mr. Beiderman didn't respond, but his eyes were very shiny, and he put one hand on Jessie's shoulder and the other on Orlando's before Laney hugged him again and made him go through the maze with her four times.

Oliver walked over to Herman, who was adjusting the yarn-bomb pieces on the fence while everyone else was exclaiming over the plants and admiring the lavender maze.

"The garden lives to see another day," Oliver said to him.

Herman nodded, and they watched as people discovered the lavender maze and exclaimed over the music.

"I wonder who gave us all those lavender plants," Oliver said.

Herman smiled, and something about it made a light bulb turn on in Oliver's brain. "Hey, was it *you* who left all those lavender plants and rosebushes by the gate?"

Herman shrugged and went back to fussing with the yarn flowers. "Yeah, so?"

"But that must have been expensive!" Oliver said. "We know because we looked it up online. I mean, those plants must have cost more than your—" He paused midsentence and glanced past the gate. He had gotten so used to seeing Herman's bike leaning against the fence that now the spot looked so empty and all wrong. "Oh," he finished.

"It's fine," Herman said. "I wanted to do it."

Oliver paused. "Well, I have to start saving up again for my own bike, since my money . . . well, I used it for something else. We can do some jobs together to earn money. You're okay cleaning toilets, right?"

"Only if we can get matching bikes," Herman said, a smile filling his face.

"Of course," Oliver said. He stuck out his hand, and Herman smiled and shook it.

❖ ❖ ❖

Jessie, Orlando, and Isa were hanging around the lavender maze, watching delighted people engage the sensor and start the orchestra music going. Off to the side, Jessie noticed a balloon with the string tangled in the tree limb of the big silver maple.

"How did that balloon get there?" she asked Orlando and Isa.

They shrugged and followed her. "You cannot believe how much trash we pulled out of this lot," Jessie said to her sister. "It could have filled a whole dumpster. I have made it my personal mission to keep this lot *absolutely* trash free."

Jessie reached the tree and noticed an envelope attached to the bottom of the balloon string.

The envelope had her name on it. She looked at Isa and Orlando. "What is this?"

Orlando and Isa exchanged looks, and then Oliver and Mr. Beiderman and the rest of her family drifted over.

"I WONDER WHAT THAT IS!" Laney squealed, jumping up and down. "I DON'T KNOW WHAT IT COULD BE!"

"Read it out loud!" Isa said.

Jessie raised an eyebrow at everyone before pulling off the envelope and opening it. She read it out loud. "'Dear Jessie, We are so glad you will be joining us for our twenty-second year of science camp. Enclosed is a packing list, as well as an overview of the scientific theories we will be exploring. The camp will culminate in a special project . . .'" Jessie stopped reading and looked up. "But—what—How did—I'm so—What?"

Everyone laughed, and Laney couldn't hold it in anymore. "You're going to science camp! You're going to science camp!" she chanted.

"How did you know?" Jessie asked Isa.

Isa smiled and pointed at Oliver. "It was his idea."

Jessie looked shocked. "Really?" she asked.

"No biggie," Oliver said, jumping up to grab a tree branch and swinging from it. "I found that letter saying you got in—"

Jessie's eyes narrowed, but Oliver hurried on.

"—and Mr. Beiderman and I called to see if there was still space for you, and they'd just had a cancellation, so a bunch of us pitched in to pay for room and board and now you get to go."

"I wish you had told us about the camp back when you first got in," Isa told Jessie.

Jessie shrugged. "I wasn't that excited about it."

Mr. Beiderman plucked the letter from Jessie's hand. "So I should tell them you don't want to go?"

Jessie grabbed the letter back, then smoothed out the wrinkles. "Don't you dare."

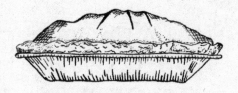

Epilogue
Three months later

I think my pumpkin will be the biggest."

"What are we going to do with all this zucchini?"

"Do you think Mama is going to win the best pie competition?"

The Vanderbeekers, along with what seemed like everyone else on 141st Street, were milling around the garden. Isa and Benny were examining the pie selections (Mama had made ten, and everyone felt bad for the rest of the competition). Laney was forcing Mr. Jeet and Miss Josie to inspect every single pumpkin in the pumpkin contest (everyone knew that Laney's huge pumpkin, which she had grown between the Silver Queen and Tilia of the Eternal Spring, was going to win). Jessie and Orlando were unsuccessfully

HARVEST FESTIVAL!

Saturday, October 5th
3 pm - 6 pm

Games!   Pie Competition!
Food!   Pumpkin Contest!
Dance-off!

bobbing for apples and laughing hysterically ("Do you think that's sanitary?" Mr. Beiderman had asked them). Hyacinth, Herman, and Mr. Jones the postman were decorating Tilia of the Eternal Spring with tiny knitted pumpkins and spiders. Mama and Auntie

Harrigan were fussing with the food tables, refilling bowls and rearranging the food to facilitate optimal traffic flow. Oliver, Angie, and Jimmy L were selling cups of apple cider; Mr. Beiderman insisted that all proceeds go toward buying spring bulbs they could put into the ground before the first frost.

Two months ago, Jessie and Orlando had changed up the musical selection in the lavender maze. It now played a mix of classical music, since everyone except Isa and Mr. Beiderman was getting tired of hearing "Roses from the South" over and over again. But at the moment, no one could hear it because Uncle Arthur had connected speakers to his phone and was playing pop songs, and lots of people were dancing in a grassy area surrounding Luciana's flowers, which were still blooming and were the centerpiece of the garden.

To call everyone's attention for the Harvest Festival speeches—which the Vanderbeeker kids had rehearsed for the past week—Uncle Arthur switched off the music and Isa took out her violin and started playing a snazzy jig she had learned from her friends at orchestra camp.

Her violin drew a crowd the same way Mama's

baking did. When Isa struck the last chord with a flourish, Hyacinth and Herman stepped up to Mr. Jeet and Miss Josie and draped them with yarn necklaces they had made.

"Thank you all for coming to our very first Harvest Celebration," Jessie began.

"Today we'd like to dedicate this garden . . ." Oliver said.

". . . to our very wonderful neighbors . . ." Isa continued.

". . . who started us on this journey in the first place," Jessie finished.

There was a pause, and everyone looked at one another and raised their eyebrows; then Oliver hissed, "Laney, that's *your* cue!"

Laney, who had gotten distracted watching a squirrel attempt to steal a piece of pie, jumped up and ran to Mr. Jeet and Miss Josie, who were seated on folding chairs. She gathered two ropes attached to a bedsheet and gave one end to Mr. Jeet and one end to Miss Josie.

"If you need help pulling, just let me know," Laney said.

Mr. Jeet gestured for her to grab hold of his rope,

and Hyacinth offered to help Miss Josie, and on the count of three, they pulled down the sheet, which fell on Franz and caused him to yelp and run in circles until Oliver stepped on one of the ropes and the sheet slid off the dog's back.

A cheer rose into the air when everyone saw the sign. Then half the crowd gathered around to wait their turn to hug Mr. Jeet and Miss Josie, while the other half went to rescue the pies from being stolen by the squirrel. Uncle Arthur put the music back on, and the Vanderbeekers had a few moments to stand back and observe the garden, watch their friends and family, and think about all they had accomplished over the summer.

"A garden should always have a party in it," Jessie said to her siblings, who stood around her to admire the sign.

"Very poetic," Isa said approvingly.

"Who said that?" Oliver asked suspiciously. "Not that Audrey Hepburn person, right?"

"Nope. Just me," Jessie said.

"You should write that on a card and tie it up to the fence," Hyacinth suggested, pointing to the dozens of quote cards the neighbors had contributed to the fence in the past three months.

"Maybe I will," Jessie replied.

And she did. As it turned out, all the Vanderbeekers had something to say.

A garden should always have a party in it. -Jessie

Keep calm and garden on! -Oliver

Happiness is spending a day in the garden with friends. ~Hyacinth♡

Music makes a garden bloom.♪ -Isa

BEING IN A gArden MAKES ME WANT TO dANCE! -LANEy

Acknowledgments

A finished book is a kind of magic, and I'm so grateful to everyone at Houghton Mifflin Harcourt Books for Young Readers for making this magic happen. First I have to thank Ann Rider, my wonderful editor, for loving the Vanderbeekers as much as I do. Ann's editorial eye, combined with her intuition and kindness, has made this book a complete joy to write. Tara Shanahan is the best (and most punctual!) publicist ever, and I will gladly travel the country with her anytime. Thanks to Lisa Vega for the beautiful book design, and to the wonderful Lisa DiSarro and Amanda Acevedo for their hard work putting the Vanderbeekers into the hands of teachers and librarians. A shout-out to Alia Almeida and to all the HMH sales reps who travel miles and miles to share books with booksellers. I'm incredibly grateful to Cat Onder, Mary Wilcox, Karen Walsh, Lily Kessinger, Mary Magrisso, Lauren Cepero, Candace Finn, Elizabeth Agyemang, and Kristin Brodeur for their wonderful support for me and this book. Many thanks to Colleen Fellingham and Alix Redmond for their meticulous copyediting, and a huge hug to Karl James Mountford for another stunningly gorgeous book cover and to map illustrator Jennifer Thermes for making the Vanderbeekers' neighborhood so inviting and lovely.

My Curtis Brown family has provided so much enthusiasm and support every step of the way. I don't know what I would do without my agent Ginger Clark, and I dedicate the wombat reference in this book to her. A basket of adorable puppies goes to Tess Callero, and a flourishing vegetable harvest to Holly Frederick, the first person at Curtis Brown to read about the Vanderbeeker family and to believe in their story.

Librarians, teachers, booksellers, readers—thank

you for welcoming the Vanderbeekers into your lives and for spreading the word about them. It means the world to me!

An author needs writer friends, and I have an embarrassment of riches in that area. My writing partner, Janice Nimura, offers endless encouragement, lunch, and chocolate. I am grateful to my middle grade critique partners, Laura Shovan, Casey Lyall, Timanda Wertz, and Margaret Dilloway, who read early drafts of this book and gave invaluable feedback. The community of Kid Lit writers is unbelievable, and I am incredibly thankful to Linda Sue Park, Linda Urban, Jennifer Chambliss Bertman, the incredible 2017 debut group, and so many others who have supported this book and provided excellent counsel along the way.

A special thanks to Lauren Hart, my dear friend, who reads every draft and provides daily encouragement and love. I am also grateful to Emily Rabin, Katie Graves-Abe, Desiree Welsing, Michael Glaser, and Kathleen Glaser for always being ready to help in any way they can.

A huge thanks to the many communities that inspire and encourage me, including the Town School, the

Town School Book Club, Book Riot, the New York Society Library, the New York Public Library, the Book Cellar, the Lucy Moses School, and my Harlem neighbors.

Finally, this dream job of writing children's books is only because of the loving support of my family: Dan, Kaela, and Lina. They make my world go round.

Turn the page for a sneak peek of

THE VANDERBEEKERS
to the RESCUE

It's springtime in Harlem, and the Vanderbeeker kids have one glorious week off from school. Their plans include preparing for a high-stakes violin audition (Isa), working on the best science fair project ever (Jessie), building the treehouse of his dreams (Oliver), knitting a pair of house slippers for Franz (Hyacinth), and practicing flips (Laney). Their plans do *not* include singlehandedly destroying Mama's baking business. While the kids race against the clock to fix their epic mistake, they realize that nothing is as easy as it seems, especially when mysterious packages arrive at their door and threaten to ruin everything.

In this third book in the Vanderbeeker series, revisit the warmth of the brownstone on 141st Street and watch the Vanderbeekers bring a little more joy and kindness to the neighborhood, one hilarious, impossible plan at a time.

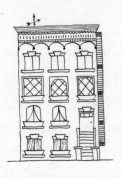

One

It was a blustery, wintry afternoon on 141st Street. A blizzard was ripping up the East Coast, and the center of the storm had decided to stay on top of Harlem and hang out for a while. Meanwhile, the brownstones along the street stood strong and steady, protecting their inhabitants the same way they had for over a hundred years. While plows rumbled up and down the avenues, snow inched up the windowsills and dusted the bricks, engulfing parked cars and piling up on sidewalks.

In the exact middle of 141st Street sat a humble red brownstone with a weathervane currently covered in snow. The Vanderbeeker family lived on the ground and first floors of this brownstone, and at the moment they were all in the living room. Thirteen-year-old twins Jessie and Isa, ten-year-old Oliver, and eight-year-old Hyacinth were regretting that they had let Laney, newly turned six, choose the board game. She had selected the very one that could go on for hours. As they waited their turn to roll the dice, each yearned for warmer weather, spring bulbs peeking up through the earth, and getting dirty in the community garden they had created for their upstairs neighbors the year before.

When her phone rang, Mama weaved through kids, pets, and stacks of books to grab it from the side table by the door. The Vanderbeekers heard her say "Really?" and "Of course!" and "That would be wonderful!" As her voice grew in volume and enthusiasm, the Vanderbeeker kids paused from their game.

Papa, who was wearing his favorite pair of forest-green coveralls and attempting to fix a leak in the kitchen sink, put down his wrench and made his way toward Mama to see what was going on. When she hung up, her whole family was surrounding her. Her eyes were bright with a mixture of excitement and astonishment.

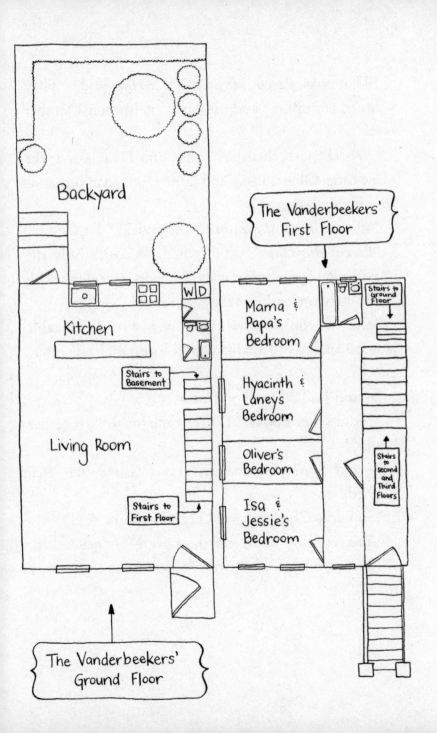

"That was *Perch Magazine*," Mama said. "They want to feature me and my business in their October issue."

"What?" screeched Isa, Jessie, and Hyacinth at the same time. Oliver, Papa, and Laney looked at one another in confusion.

"What's *Birch Magazine*?" Oliver said.

"*Perch Magazine*," Isa clarified. "And it's only the most amazing magazine ever. They do interviews with awesome women, like Hope Jahren—"

"She's a geobiologist known for her work on stable isotope analysis to analyze fossil forests!" Jessie interrupted.

"—and Jacqueline Woodson—"

"I know her books!" Oliver exclaimed. "I *love* her books!"

"—and Sonia Sotomayor," Isa finished, her face flushed.

"Supreme Court justice!" Hyacinth squeaked.

"You're going to be on the cover?" Laney asked. "What are you going to wear? Can I be in the picture too?"

Mama looked dazed. "I'm definitely *not* going to be on the cover. They have a section about small-business owners, and they want to feature me. I have no idea how they even know me! Someone from the magazine must have gone to an event where my desserts were served. There will be a whole magazine spread about my cookies! They're going to send a photographer to the brownstone!"

Papa pulled Mama into a hug and started doing a little dance with her at the bottom of the stairs. "I'm so proud of you."

Jessie took out her phone, opened the web browser, and typed madly with her thumbs. "Holy smokes, listen to these circulation numbers. Eight hundred thousand print copies and over two million unique views on their website every month!"

"You're going to be famous!" Laney yelled, hopping around them.

"Now *everyone* is going to want your cookies," Oliver said, mentally calculating how Mama's increased business might positively affect his weekly allowance.

"You're going to need a website and a wholesale list," Isa said wisely.

"How do you know that?" Jessie asked.

"Benny has to do it for Castleman's Bakery," Isa said.

"When is the photo shoot?" Papa asked.

"The first week in April," Mama said.

"That's when your birthday is!" Laney yelled. "On April sixth!"

Mama's hands flew to her cheeks as she looked around the brownstone. The Vanderbeekers followed her gaze, and suddenly they saw their home as a fancy magazine photographer might. Franz, their basset hound, was methodically removing toys from his basket and strategically placing them in areas with the most foot traffic. Hay was strewn on the floor from Paganini, Laney's rabbit, who kicked as much of it as possible when jumping out of his box. George Washington, their orange-and-white tabby, was batting at the loose threads from the fabric of their couch, which was fraying because he used the furniture to sharpen his claws (even though there were two scratching posts in the living room).

And then there were the piles of books, the odds and ends of Jessie's science experiments, and Isa's sheet music tossed on various surfaces. Oliver's basketball was wedged under an armchair, and Hyacinth's treasure box gaped open, yarn in a dozen colors spilling out in every direction.

Jessie spoke first. "We can totally make this brownstone magazine-worthy."

Oliver was skeptical. "We can?"

Isa stood up straighter. "Of course we can!"

Papa touched the living room walls. "I've been meaning to patch and paint the walls. And refinish the floors. And build some more bookcases, because obviously five huge bookcases aren't enough for us. I can do that by April."

Mama's jaw began to relax.

"Mama, trust us," Isa told her. "We've got this."

The family gathered around her and did a communal Vanderbeeker fist bump.

"Fame and fortune, here we come!" Oliver yelled.

Monday, April 1

One month, eight days later

HURSDAY	FRIDAY	SATURDAY
4	5 Perch Magazine Photo Shoot! Isa's Audition	6 Mama's Birthday!
B·R·E·A·K		

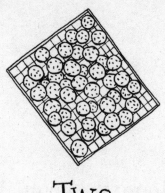

Two

It turned out that thirty-six days were not nearly enough to make the apartment magazine-ready. The past month had been full of unexpected emergencies. Laney had had her tonsils removed and lived on milkshakes and applesauce for days. Oliver had sprained two fingers while playing basketball and wore splints for three weeks, and when his fingers had healed, he'd then managed to run his bike into a tree and ended up in the emergency room for x-rays. (He was fine.) Hyacinth had come down with an ear infection, strep throat, and pinkeye at the same time. Isa and Jessie were dragging under the weight of increased homework, and Isa had also been practicing violin in the basement every day for hours in preparation for an upcoming orchestra audition. Papa had been assigned a big project and had been working late nights and weekends, and Mama had been baking nonstop in addition to doing business-related things like creating a website, developing promotional items, and preparing for the interview.

Now it was spring break, and it was a big week. There were only five days until the *Perch Magazine* photo shoot on Friday, which also happened to be the day of Isa's audition, and Mama's birthday was on Saturday. Somehow the apartment seemed even more chaotic than usual.

"We need a game plan," Isa told her siblings, who were scattered throughout the living room.

Laney was rearranging books to build a maze for Paganini. She believed mazes would make the rabbit even smarter than he already was. Hyacinth was kneeling on the floor, her eyes two inches from the carpet, trying to locate a sewing needle she had dropped. Over on the couch, Jessie was highlighting nearly every sentence in a science book she had found for fifty cents at the library sale. Oliver was staring out the window at the relentless rain and muttering to himself.

Return to Harlem in:

A *New York Times* Notable Children's Book of 2017
An American Booksellers Association Fall 2017 Indie Next Pick
A Junior Library Guild Selection
An American Booksellers Association 2017 Indies Introduce Title

"Delightful and heartwarming."
—*New York Times Book Review*

★ "A pitch-perfect debut. . . . Readers will look forward to future
adventures. A highly recommended purchase."
—*School Library Journal,* starred review

★ "Few [families] in children's literature are as engaging or
amusing as the Vanderbeekers, even in times of turmoil. . . .
A biracial family with a close-knit diverse community, the
Vanderbeekers are swiftly, deftly individualized. . . .
Beautifully written. . . . Wildly entertaining."
—*Booklist,* starred review

"Utterly enchanting."
—Linda Sue Park, Newbery medalist